Everyone loves Nanny Piggins!

Praise for *Nanny Piggins and the Wicked Plan*:

★ "Feisty, funny Nanny Piggins and her adoring charges will charm readers and listeners…" —*Kirkus* (starred review)

Praise for *The Adventures of Nanny Piggins*:

★ "Mary Poppins, move over—or get shoved out of the way. Nanny Piggins has arrived….This is smart, sly, funny, and marvelously illustrated with drawings that capture Nanny's sheer pigginess." —*Booklist* (starred review)

"Readers looking for nonstop giggles and cheerful political incorrectness will devour this as quickly as Nanny Piggins can consume a chocolate cake." —*Publishers Weekly*

"Reluctant and avid readers alike will get caught up in this book's humor, charm, and adventure." —*School Library Journal*

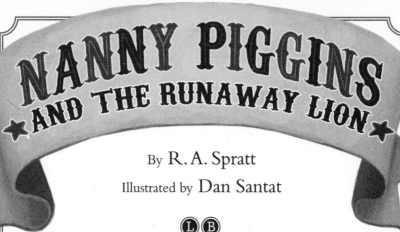

NANNY PIGGINS
AND THE RUNAWAY LION

By R. A. Spratt

Illustrated by Dan Santat

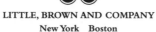

LITTLE, BROWN AND COMPANY
New York   Boston

Text copyright © 2010 by R. A. Spratt
Illustrations copyright © 2014 by Dan Santat

Little, Brown and Company

Hachette Book Group
237 Park Avenue, New York, NY 10017
Visit our website at lb-kids.com

Little, Brown and Company is a division of Hachette Book Group, Inc.
The Little, Brown name and logo are trademarks of Hachette Book Group, Inc.

The publisher is not responsible for websites (or their content) that are not owned by the publisher.

First U.S. Edition: June 2014
Originally published in 2010 by Random House Australia Pty Ltd.

Library of Congress Cataloging-in-Publication Data
Spratt, R. A.
Nanny Piggins and the runaway lion / by R. A. Spratt ; illustrated by Dan Santat. — First U.S. edition.
pages cm
Summary: "When Mr. Green tries to send Derrick, Samantha, and Michael away to school, Nanny Piggins must thwart his plan"— Provided by publisher.
ISBN 978-0-316-25453-3 (hardcover) — ISBN 978-0-316-25455-7 (electronic book) [1. Nannies—Fiction. 2. Brothers and sisters—Fiction. 3. Pigs—Fiction. 4. Humorous stories.] I. Santat, Dan, illustrator. II. Title.
PZ7.S76826Nah 2014
[Fic]—dc23

2013022830

10 9 8 7 6 5 4 3 2 1

RRD-C

Printed in the United States of America

Book design by Saho Fujii

······ **PREVIOUSLY ON NANNY PIGGINS...** ·······

IF YOU HAVE JUST PICKED UP THIS BOOK AND are wondering—Who are these characters? What's been going on? How can a pig be a nanny?—do not be daunted.

All you need to know is that Nanny Piggins (the world's most glamorous flying pig) ran away from the circus and came to live with the Green family as their nanny. The children, Derrick, Samantha, and Michael, fell in love with her instantly. Who could not love a nanny who thinks that the five major food groups are chocolate, chocolate, chocolate, more chocolate, and cake?

The Green children are lovely, normal children. Derrick can be a little scruffy and grubby, but then, isn't that true of all eleven-year-old boys? Samantha does tend to worry, but nine-year-old girls who mysteriously lose their mothers in boating accidents would be silly not to be concerned. And Michael is an uncomplicated, happy soul who shares his nanny's enthusiasm for high-sugar food.

Before long Nanny Piggins's adopted brother, Boris, the dancing bear, came to live in their garden shed (unbeknownst to Mr. Green, the children's father).

There are other recurring characters—a silly headmaster, a perfectly perfect rival nanny, thirteen identical twin sisters, a besotted School District Superintendent, and a wicked Ringmaster, just to name a few. But trust me, you will pick all that up as you go along.

The only other person you need to know about is Mr. Green. He is not happy about having a pig for a nanny, or having children generally. Secretly he would like nothing more than for Derrick, Samantha, and Michael to disappear into thin air, perhaps as part of a conjuring trick. But he realizes that is unlikely, although not impossible, because it is essentially what happened to their mother, Mrs. Green, on one very unfortunate boating trip.

Mr. Green did try to remarry in an effort to get rid of Nanny Piggins and palm his children on someone else, but that proved disastrous. (For further details, see *Nanny Piggins and the Wicked Plan*.) So as this book begins, Mr. Green is cooking up new schemes to make himself childless.

Yours sincerely,
R. A. Spratt, the author

To Mum and Dad

R.A. Spratt and Nanny Piggins
would also like to thank…

Connie Hsu
Chris Kunz
Elizabeth Troyeur
the wonderful librarians of America
and
the great indefatigable children's lit pusher of
Los Angeles, Lindy Michaels

CONTENTS

CHAPTER ONE

Nanny Piggins and the Foreign Exchange Student

an anyone remember what the figurines looked like?" asked Nanny Piggins.

"All I can remember is that they were ugly," said Boris.

Nanny Piggins, Boris, and the children were in the living room looking at the shattered remnants of the late Grandma Green's figurine collection. The ten miniature statues had accidentally been smashed in a particularly athletic game of charades. (Nanny Piggins had set a vase of flowers on fire when acting out the book title

The Bonfire of the Vanities. Then she had to leap to safety before her hair was caught in the inferno.)

"I think one of the figurines was a woman with a dog," said Michael. As a seven-year-old boy, he naturally had an affinity with dogs.

"I'm pretty sure those green parts were a mermaid," said Derrick, who, as an eleven-year-old, was developing an eye for mermaids.

"And one was a milkmaid with a cow...or a goat... but definitely something you milked," added Samantha. Being a nine-year-old who worried a lot, she did not like to commit to a decision.

"I know what we can do," said Nanny Piggins. "Let's recombine all the pieces to make one giant figurine of a monkey!"

"Why a monkey?" asked Boris.

"Everyone likes monkeys," said Nanny Piggins.

The others nodded at the truth of this statement.

"Which just goes to show," continued Nanny Piggins, "you can scratch yourself, slap your head, and bite tourists, but if you do it with enough charm, people will still think you're adorable."

So they set to work. Nanny Piggins was extremely good with superglue. When you smashed as many Ming vases as she had in her time, you needed to be. They had just reached the point where all ten of their hands were required to hold everything in place while the glue set when Mr. Green walked into the room.

"Wah!" said Boris as he ducked under the table. Then "Ow!" as he realized he had just ripped out a chunk of fur because he had accidentally superglued his paw to the figurine. Fortunately Mr. Green did not notice the ten-foot-tall dancing bear hiding under the table, because he was a very unobservant man. And the brain tends not to process information that is impossible to believe.

"Hello, children," said Mr. Green.

They all immediately knew something terrible was wrong because Mr. Green usually never spoke to the children except to tell them to "Go away" or "Be quiet" or "Stop pestering me for lunch money." Also, he was smiling, a skill he was very bad at. Mr. Green's smiles were frightening. Like a baboon baring his teeth right before he poops on his hand and throws it at you.

"Hello," said Nanny Piggins conversationally. "We were just polishing your beloved figurine. What do you think?"

Mr. Green leaned forward and peered at it. They all held their breath as they waited to see if he would notice the difference between the ten original figurines and the giant one they were now holding.

"It looks fine," said Mr. Green.

They sighed with relief.

"But..." he continued.

They held their breath again.

"Has it always been furry?" Mr. Green asked, looking at the brown tuft now stuck to the monkey's neck.

"Oh yes," said Nanny Piggins. "Embedded bear fur is the signature mark of a genuine antique Staffordshire flatback."

"Really? Well, my mother had quite the eye," said Mr. Green proudly. (It is funny how people grow fond of the relatives who once terrified them after they are safely dead.)

"Don't let us keep you from your tax law work," hinted Nanny Piggins as she politely tried to get rid of Mr. Green. "I know you must have something dreadfully important to do in your office. Paper clips to straighten and rebend, or some such."

This comment slightly unnerved Mr. Green because that was exactly what he had spent four hours doing only that morning, and then billed the time to a rich, old widow who was too nearsighted to check her invoice.

"Oh, no, I came in here to make an announcement," he said. "You children are very lucky."

The children groaned. They knew something terrible was coming if their father thought they were lucky.

"What have you done?" Nanny Piggins glowered, suspecting him of trying to sell them for medical experiments again. "The hospital told you clearly. They don't accept donated organs from living people."

"No, this is another, even better, idea. I've arranged a wonderful educational opportunity for the three of you," continued Mr. Green. He really was beginning to look very smug.

"What sort of wonderful educational opportunity?" asked Nanny Piggins, bracing herself to launch, teeth-first, at his leg.

"Well, you see, a fellow at work was telling me about

his son and how he sent him away as an exchange student," said Mr. Green.

"And how does that affect Derrick, Samantha, and Michael?" asked Nanny Piggins suspiciously.

"I thought it sounded like such a good idea I've enrolled them in an exchange-student program!" said Mr. Green triumphantly, whipping the paperwork out of his pocket and waving it in their faces. "It's all arranged. By the end of next week, they'll be off to Nicaragua for six months." Mr. Green was positively glowing with happiness. The idea of six months without his own children pleased him immensely.

"But I don't want to go to Nicaragua!" protested Nanny Piggins. "I've been there twice already, and while the turtles are nice and *gallo pinto* is delicious, the humid weather makes it very difficult to do anything with my hair."

"*You* won't be going," said Mr. Green.

"But what will Nanny Piggins do while we're away?" worried Samantha.

"Find a new job, of course," said Mr. Green.

"Noooooo!" yelled Michael. Being the youngest,

he was more prone to outbursts of emotion. He would have flung himself at his father in a rage, but, like Boris, he had accidentally glued his hands to the figurine.

And Derrick tried to kick his father's shin under the table. Unfortunately, as he was only eleven years old, his legs weren't long enough to reach.

"I'm sure Miss Piggins will find work somewhere else," said Mr. Green. "Perhaps"—he started to laugh here as though he had thought of something funny—"perhaps she can get a job"—again he actually chortled—"in a bacon factory."

The children gasped and Boris banged his head on the dining table as he flinched away in horror. There was no greater insult to a pig than to mention the word *bacon*. Mr. Green's idea of a joke had mortally offended Nanny Piggins. If it were not for the fact that she, like Michael and Boris, had too much superglue on her trotters and was now stuck to the figurine, Mr. Green would have been in terrible trouble. As it was, she dragged the giant figurine three feet across the table as she lunged toward him.

Mr. Green cowered away. "It is all legitimate. Lots

of parents do it. It's educational," he protested, the way people always protest when they have done something very bad and are about to be punished for it.

"I suggest you leave the room now, Mr. Green," said Nanny Piggins, "to allow the children and me time to control our emotions."

Emotions of all varieties scared Mr. Green, so he did as he was told. He scuttled away and drove back to the office.

"What are we going to do?" wailed Samantha. She was not normally given to wailing, but the prospect of six months in Nicaragua can have that effect on a girl.

"Obviously we will have to thwart your father," said Nanny Piggins. "It really is exhausting putting him in his place all the time. I wonder if we got him a futon whether we could persuade him to sleep in his office and never come home."

"Do you have a plan?" asked Michael hopefully. He would actually have quite liked to go to Nicaragua because he was an adventurous boy who was, of course, intrigued by turtles. But he did not want to be separated from Nanny Piggins. She was the only family the children had. If you did not count their father. And none of them did.

"I have the beginning of an idea," admitted Nanny

Piggins as she thoughtfully rubbed her snout. (She had to rub it on her arm because, of course, her trotters were glued to the figurine.)

"What do we have to do?" asked Derrick, desperate to take some sort of action.

"Well, for a start, we have to resmash this figurine," said Nanny Piggins.

"To teach Father a lesson?" asked Samantha.

"That is an added benefit. But the main reason is because we're all stuck to it. And I've run out of nail polish remover, so I've got nothing to dissolve the glue," said Nanny Piggins.

So after smashing the figurine back into a thousand pieces, and leaving it there because Mr. Green did not deserve to have it refixed, the children went off to school. Nanny Piggins assured them that she would soon solve the problem. Two weeks was a lot of time. She was sure to think of something.

The family was sitting around the breakfast table the next morning, which was not a pleasant experience for

Mr. Green. He kept getting hit in the head with slices of toast. Michael claimed they were slipping out of his hands when he buttered them, but Mr. Green suspected that his youngest son might have been throwing them intentionally. Suddenly, there was a knock at the front door.

"Who could that be?" demanded Mr. Green.

"I expect it is someone at the front door," explained Nanny Piggins slowly and clearly. "They probably want you to open the door and speak to them."

"One of you children go," said Mr. Green dismissively.

"The children shouldn't answer the door to strangers," chided Nanny Piggins.

"Then you answer it," said Mr. Green.

"Very well," said Nanny Piggins, primping her hair as she got up from the table. "But if it is someone important who has come to give you a medal for services to tax law, are you sure you want the door to be answered by a pig, even if she is the most glamorous pig in the entire world?"

"All right, I'll do it myself," grumbled Mr. Green. As far as he was concerned, the fewer people who knew he housed a pig the better. Little did he realize, however, that while a great number of people knew Nanny Piggins lived in the house, almost no one knew (or cared) whether Mr. Green even existed.

Nanny Piggins and the children followed him, curious to see who would pay Mr. Green a visit at breakfast time.

Mr. Green flung open the front door. "What do you want?" he demanded rudely. Then he immediately had to look down because the person he was being rude to was two feet shorter than he was expecting.

"Bonjour, Monsieur Green," said the diminutive boy standing on the doorstep. "My name is François. I am eleven years old and from Belgium. And I am to be your exchange student. It is a great pleasure to be welcomed to your country!" François then reached up, grabbed Mr. Green's head, pulled him down, and kissed him once on each cheek.

Mr. Green practically went into shock as François picked up his little suitcase and entered the house.

"Bonjour, I am François," François said to Nanny Piggins and the Green children.

"Bonjour," said Derrick, Samantha, and Michael.

"Thank you for welcoming me into your home," continued François with impeccable politeness and a lovely little bow. "I look forward to immersing myself in your culture."

"What does 'immerse yourself in culture' mean?" Michael whispered to Derrick.

"I think he wants to dip himself in yogurt," Derrick guessed.

"Now just you wait here," spluttered Mr. Green. "What is the meaning of this? Coming into my house with a suitcase and speaking French. It just isn't acceptable."

"But you are Mr. Green, yes?" asked François, looking just the right amount of confused and hurt to make even Mr. Green feel slightly guilty for raising his voice.

"Well, yes," admitted Mr. Green, secretly wishing he was not.

"And you signed up to join the Friends Around the World exchange-student program, did you not?" François asked.

"He did indeed," said Nanny Piggins. "We all saw the paperwork yesterday."

"Yes, but that was to send my children *away*," protested Mr. Green.

"Of course," said François. "But before your children go, you must first host a student in your home. That is the way the system works. Didn't you read the fine print of the contract?"

Mr. Green had not. Which was unusual because he was a lawyer and it was his job to write fine print into contracts. So he should have known better than anyone how devious fine print can be. But when he was at the exchange-student office, he had been so euphoric at the idea of six months without his children he had been too giddy for reading. Instead he had been busily fantasizing about closing up the children's bedrooms and saving money by disconnecting the electricity to all but one room in the house.

"How long are you going to be here?" asked Mr. Green, beginning to accept that perhaps there was no way out of this predicament. "Not six months, I hope."

"*Non, non, non,*" said François (which is French for "no, no, no"). "I will be here for twelve months. I am on the advanced program."

"Twelve months!" exclaimed Mr. Green, truly aghast. "But what am I supposed to do with you?"

"Just treat me as you would your own children," said François.

"He's going to wish he stayed in Belgium," predicted Michael under his breath.

Mr. Green would have dearly loved to send François packing, but after fetching the contract and reading the fine print three times, he realized he could not. If he wanted his children to go to Nicaragua, he had to host the Belgian boy. But Mr. Green reasoned that one foreign child had to be better than three of his own (it was just a case of simple mathematics to his mind), so he decided to stick to his decision. Once Derrick, Samantha, and Michael were safely in Nicaragua, perhaps there would be some way he could lend François out to a sweatshop or a chimney-sweeping service or some such.

The next few days proved very interesting. François was a polite, charming little boy who went to his own international school in town. So he was no bother for Nanny Piggins, Boris, and the children at all. But for some reason, he was fascinated by Mr. Green.

He kept muttering things like, "*Sacre bleu!* (which is French for "Wow!") We have no one like this in our country."

Every time Mr. Green slurped his soup, picked his nose, or dug the wax out of his ear, François would be there taking notes and even drawing diagrams, which he would then delightedly take and show the other children.

"Observe your father. He is a most fascinating man," exclaimed François.

"He is?" asked Derrick, not entirely convinced.

"Oh yes, there is none other like him, I think. I must document all his behavior to show the people back in Belgium or they would not believe it," said François happily.

"You should get a tape recorder," suggested Nanny Piggins, "so you can capture the noises he makes in his natural habitat." She liked to encourage children, particularly ones with such a talent for irritating Mr. Green.

"*Très bien*, what a good idea!" exclaimed François. "I shall purchase one now."

"You will not," protested Mr. Green.

"Tsk, tsk, Mr. Green," chided Nanny Piggins. "You

don't want to cause an international incident. François is only trying to learn about our culture."

But Mr. Green could not bear it. Whenever he was home, François followed him about, pestering him with questions all day long. "Why do you comb your hair over your bald spot?" "Are you ashamed of your head?" "Why are you ashamed of your head?" "Do you have a rude tattoo up there?" "What does it say?" "Can't you afford to buy new clothes?" "Where do you get your suits from?" "Do you buy them from widows whose husbands have just died?" "Have you ever thought about plucking your nose hair?" "Would you like to borrow my tweezers?"

And Mr. Green could not do what he did to avoid his regular children—go to the office—because François's school encouraged his sociological research by giving him time off to follow Mr. Green around at work too.

Everyone at the law offices loved François, which only irritated Mr. Green even more. The secretaries all wanted to see François's diagrams of Mr. Green and the earwax. And even the senior partners had a good chortle when François played them the recordings he made of Mr. Green getting into and out of a chair. As a result,

François had only been staying with them for two days when Nanny Piggins found Mr. Green hiding behind a bush down at the far end of the garden.

"Are you doing a spot of pruning?" asked Nanny Piggins innocently.

"Is that boy anywhere nearby?" whispered Mr. Green.

"What boy?" asked Nanny Piggins loudly.

"Shhh, he'll hear you," said Mr. Green. "François. Is he about? Is it safe for me to come out?"

"Of course," said Nanny Piggins. "He isn't here. He's up in your bedroom going through your closet, taking photographs. He says the university in Brussels wants him to document everything."

"Oh dear," moaned Mr. Green.

"Are you coming in for lunch?" asked Nanny Piggins.

"No, I'll just stay here," said Mr. Green sadly. "I'll sneak back in tonight after the little . . . tyke has gone to bed."

But Mr. Green had underestimated François's dedication to his study. Later that night, the children were woken up by the sound of their father screaming. They rushed to his room. Not so much because they wanted to help but because, if their father was finally going to snap and throw a tantrum, they wanted to see it for themselves.

"Get him out! Get him out!" screamed Mr. Green.

"But what have I done wrong?" asked François, looking the picture of innocence.

"I woke up, and he was standing over me, holding a flashlight with a video camera," complained Mr. Green.

"Perhaps the boy had trouble sleeping," suggested Nanny Piggins.

"Monsieur Green is so fascinating when he slumbers," explained François. "He makes exactly the same noise as a wildebeest with its foot stuck in an anthill."

"Of course, you're right. I've never been able to put my trotter on it," agreed Nanny Piggins, "but that's the sound exactly."

"I want this boy out of my house now!" yelled Mr. Green.

"Very well," said François with a hurt look on his little face. "I don't want to be where I'm not wanted." His lip quivered, and he fled from the room.

"Monsieur Green is so fascinating when he slumbers," explained François.

The children were even more ashamed of their father than usual.

"But if he goes, Derrick, Samantha, and Michael won't be able to go to Nicaragua next week," protested Nanny Piggins.

"I don't care," said Mr. Green. (He did care, but he was so deranged from lack of sleep that he had forgotten.)

"And if Derrick, Samantha, and Michael stay, who will take care of them? I'm due to start work at the bacon factory on Monday," said Nanny Piggins, looking the picture of concern.

"Quit your job! You have to stay. I can't bear it!" exclaimed Mr. Green.

"I would," said Nanny Piggins, "but the bacon factory pays so well. It would be a step backward for me to go back to being a nanny."

"What do you want? A pay raise? Fine, I'll double your wages," said Mr. Green, which shows how desperate he was because he hated parting with money.

"No, I don't want to be paid more," said Nanny Piggins. "I am not a greedy pig. Ten cents an hour is plenty. No, I just want a weekly chocolate allowance."

"A what?" asked Mr. Green.

"A weekly allowance to cover all my chocolate expenses. The bacon factory doesn't give me that," explained Nanny Piggins. "For a chocolate allowance I just might stay."

"All right, I agree," said Mr. Green. "How much do you want?"

"Fifty dollars ought to cover it," said Nanny Piggins.

"What?!" exploded Mr. Green.

"You're right," said Nanny Piggins. "That is ridiculous. Better make it sixty."

Mr. Green was so angry at this point that he lost the ability to make coherent sentences. He spluttered and blathered random sounds like "wha...nnggg... rggrrrrr."

"Father, perhaps you'd better agree to Nanny Piggins's request," said Derrick. "Just consider the alternative."

"Remember what it was like when you had to look after us yourself," added Samantha.

Mr. Green shuddered. The pre–Nanny Piggins years had been a painful experience for him. Having to spend thirty or forty minutes with his children every day, sitting in the same room as them while they ate their meals, talking to them, and making eye contact—it was too dreadful to recall.

"All right, I agree to it all," said Mr. Green.

"Excellent," said Nanny Piggins. "There's no need to write me a check, I'll just take the money out of your wallet when you're asleep sometime."

"You'll what?" said Mr. Green.

"Don't worry, I'm much better at sneaking about a dark room than François," Nanny Piggins assured him. "You never wake up when I do it."

And so Nanny Piggins and the children left Mr. Green to get some sleep. (He locked the door and put a chair under the handle—as if that would stop a flying pig.)

Then they went downstairs to drink hot chocolate and plan how they were going to spend their newfound chocolate allowance. They were just in the middle of a heated debate over the comparative merits of chocolate malt balls and chocolate caramels when François entered.

"François!" exclaimed Samantha. "Are you all right?"

"We're sorry Father was so rude," added Derrick.

"He's not racist. He's mean to people of every nationality equally," Michael assured him.

"Don't worry about it, ay," said François in a broad Canadian accent.

"François?" said Samantha.

"You can call him Frank," said Nanny Piggins. "That's his real name."

"You two know each other?!" exclaimed Derrick.

"Oh yes," said Nanny Piggins. "You didn't think someone so uniquely irritating solely to Mr. Green could move in here just through pure coincidence, did you?"

The three children felt a little silly, realizing that that is exactly what they had thought.

"Frank isn't an eleven-year-old Belgian boy," explained Nanny Piggins. "He's a thirty-seven-year-old Canadian acrobat from the circus."

"I'm the guy who stands at the top of the human pyramid," explained Frank.

"Have you ever been dropped on your head?" asked Michael in fascination.

"All the time. You don't get reliable staff in human pyramids like you used to. These days, all the really good human pyramiders are running hedge funds," said Frank sadly.

"They are?" said Derrick.

"Yes, it's the same skill set, you see. It's all about keeping everything up in the air. And if one thing goes, the whole lot comes tumbling down on your head," explained Frank.

"Thank you for all your help," said Nanny Piggins. "We've really enjoyed having you here. If there is ever anything we can do for you in return..."

"No, it's my pleasure," said Frank. "I owed you one for that time I forgot my passport and you blasted me across the Bering Strait with your cannon."

And so Frank went back to the circus and life in the Green household returned to normal. The children remained safe in the knowledge that if they ever did visit the turtles of Nicaragua, it would be voluntarily, and at a time of their own choosing.

CHAPTER TWO

Nanny Piggins Joins the Neighborhood Watch

It was the middle of the night and Nanny Piggins was standing alone in the dark, in the middle of the front garden. But do not worry; nothing bad was happening—quite the contrary. Nanny Piggins was playing a wonderful game of Spotlight with the children.

To play Spotlight, everyone has to dress in black, then smear camouflage paint (or milk chocolate) all over their faces and hands. Then one person stands in the middle of the yard with a flashlight while everyone else hides in the dark bushes. The idea is to rush up and tag the person holding the flashlight before they can spot you.

Nanny Piggins was incredibly good at this game as, indeed, she was at most games, because she had a huge advantage. Her sense of smell was so good she could sniff anyone coming even with her eyes closed. So she could easily detect Michael trying to sneak up on her from behind. She was just about to spin around and shine the flashlight in his face when, from somewhere down the street, she heard a noise.

"What was that?" asked Nanny Piggins at the precise moment when Michael launched himself at her. Nanny Piggins stepped sideways to have a look down the street. As a result, Michael missed her and crash-tackled Derrick, who was running forward to tag his nanny from the front. Then Samantha landed on top of them both because she had climbed a tree so she could drop on Nanny Piggins from above.

"Shhh," said Nanny Piggins, as the children picked themselves up. "There's something going on down the street."

"But it's three o'clock in the morning," said Derrick disapprovingly.

"And it's a school night," said Samantha even more disapprovingly.

"Exactly," said Nanny Piggins. "There can be no good reason for anyone to be out on the street at this hour."

"Unless they're playing Spotlight with their nanny," suggested Michael.

"I doubt that's the case," said Nanny Piggins. "Other nannies do not seem to share my dedication to duty. They always want to sleep at night, whereas I see the job as a twenty-four-hour responsibility."

Nanny Piggins and the children peered down the street where they could see flashlights blinking about and could hear the low murmur of voices.

"It could just be people coming home late," said Samantha.

"In this neighborhood?!" scoffed Nanny Piggins. "All the people who live here are too boring. They're all in bed by ten thirty. I know that for a fact because when I knock on their doors asking to borrow some chocolate at one o'clock in the morning they always have to get out of bed to come and give it to me. No, it's obviously a gang of burglars."

"Should we call the police?" asked Derrick.

"I suppose," said Nanny Piggins begrudgingly. "Though I don't see why they should get to hog all the fun."

"You know the Police Sergeant doesn't like it when you make citizen's arrests," Samantha reminded her nanny.

"Yes, he is a spoilsport," agreed Nanny Piggins. (Nanny Piggins had not forgiven the Police Sergeant for telling her off after she brought into the police station a woman she had citizen's-arrested for wearing shoes that did not match her handbag.) "Michael, you run into the house and phone the police."

Michael ran back inside. Nanny Piggins turned to Derrick and Samantha. "Obviously we can't let the burglars get away before the police get here, so we'll just set up an ambush."

"I can't ambush anyone! I'm only nine," protested Samantha.

"That's why I'm giving you the most important job," said Nanny Piggins. "It's your responsibility to hold all my chocolate while I climb the tree and drop on them. It would be terrible if someone got burgled. But the real tragedy would be if something happened to my chocolate bars."

So Samantha minded the twenty-seven chocolate bars her nanny had stashed about her person while Nanny Piggins shinnied up the tree. Once she was in position, Nanny Piggins called back down. "Now, Derrick, when they come up the street you step out in front of them and ask them for directions to the cinema, then I'll take care of the rest."

The gang of burglars slowly made their way up the road, shining their flashlights into people's gardens and muttering among themselves.

"They're nearly here," whispered Derrick.

"I think I'm going to faint," whispered Samantha.

"Eat one of the chocolate bars," advised Nanny Piggins.

The burglars drew alongside the Green house and shone their flashlights about the yard.

"Now!" hissed Nanny Piggins.

Derrick leaped out of the bush and onto the sidewalk saying, "Good evening, I was wondering if you could tell me the way to the nearest—"

"Heeeeyaiiiyaaaahhhhh!" screamed Nanny Piggins as

"Heeeeyaiiiyaaaahhhhh!"
screamed Nanny Piggins.

she threw herself out of Mr. Green's tree and knocked the whole gang of burglars down, like a strike in bowling. "I am arresting you on behalf of the citizens of this street! You naughty burglars, you should be thoroughly ashamed of yourselves for breaking into people's homes at three o'clock in the morning. And on a school night too!"

"Weemmffffmmf," said one of the burglars. It was hard to understand what he was saying because his face was pressed into the sidewalk and Nanny Piggins was sitting on his back.

"I think that burglar is trying to tell you something," said Samantha as she ate a second chocolate bar in an attempt to keep her hysterics at bay.

"They probably want to bribe us with a cut of their loot," said Nanny Piggins knowledgeably, "so we should hear them out, just in case they've recently broken into a cake factory."

Nanny Piggins got to her feet, which allowed the burglars the opportunity to sit up. There were three of them: one woman and two men. They were all smartly dressed and, surprisingly, they were all over the age of sixty.

"Gosh," said Derrick. "I never knew burglars could be so old."

Nanny Piggins stood over the would-be thieves and gave them a piece of her mind. "Shame on you! At your age you shouldn't be breaking into houses. You should be committing more genteel crimes, such as fraud."

"But we're not burglars," said the elderly woman.

"That's what all burglars say," said Nanny Piggins, rolling her eyes.

"We're the local Neighborhood Watch patrol," said one of the elderly men.

"I don't care what your gang is called," said Nanny Piggins. "I'm not impressed."

"Um...Nanny Piggins," interrupted Derrick. "The Neighborhood Watch isn't a gang. It's a group for community-minded people who patrol the streets and watch their neighbors' houses."

"Burglars *and* Peeping Toms. This gets worse and worse," said Nanny Piggins.

"No, we're trying to *stop* burglars," explained the elderly woman.

"So I'm not going to get to make a citizen's arrest?" asked a disappointed Nanny Piggins.

"No," said Derrick.

"What a relief," said Samantha as she finished off her fourth chocolate bar.

The three members of the Neighborhood Watch patrol got to their feet, which took some time and a certain amount of groaning, because they were old.

"We could use a pig like you on the Neighborhood Watch," said the elderly woman. "I'm Valerie Darvas, captain of the local branch. This is Tom and Stanley."

Nanny Piggins shook hands with them all.

"No hard feelings about me smashing you into the sidewalk, then?" asked Nanny Piggins.

"Not at all," said Valerie. "It's good to meet a resident who is prepared to really tackle crime. And being ambushed from time to time is excellent training. It keeps us on our toes."

"You should come along to our next Neighborhood Watch meeting," suggested Stanley.

"I don't know," said Nanny Piggins. "I don't approve of organizations."

"If you join, you get a free flashlight," said Tom.

"Hmm," said Nanny Piggins. She did like flashlights.

"And we're having a self-defense lesson this week," added Stanley.

"Will there be wrestling?" asked Nanny Piggins.

"I should think so," said Valerie.

"Then we'll be there!" exclaimed Nanny Piggins.

Nanny Piggins was just about to shake Valerie's hand again when the police arrived and arrested them all. (Mrs. McGill, their unpleasant next-door neighbor, had called the police and reported them all for wrestling in a public street.) Nanny Piggins eventually got them all released by using the police station kitchen to bake a cake. The police soon agreed that anyone who made such a light, fluffy, and delicious sponge cake could not be a criminal, and let them all go.

Nanny Piggins was very excited when she took the children along to the Neighborhood Watch meeting that Wednesday night. She had worn her hot-pink Lycra wrestling leotard in anticipation. (Nanny Piggins owned this spectacular piece of clothing because she had enjoyed a brief stint as a professional wrestler during her time at the circus. But she had to go back to being blasted out of a cannon after just two short weeks, because she ran out of people willing to wrestle her. Even the Strong Man was no match for her flying leg lock or chomping teeth hold.) Nanny Piggins had brought Boris along as well. He was not as good at wrestling as his sister, but he was very good at sitting on people until it was their turn to be wrestled.

So Nanny Piggins was rather disappointed when she arrived and discovered that the Neighborhood Watch consisted of a room full of middle-aged and elderly concerned citizens, many of them wearing cardigans.

"Do you think they're wearing wrestling leotards under their cardigans?" asked Nanny Piggins hopefully.

"From the look of these people, you'd have to wrestle them to get them to take their cardigans off," said Boris.

Even the self-defense instructor was unimpressive. He was a slightly overweight man of about fifty who taught techniques that emphasized avoiding violence, not instigating it.

"But attack is the best defense!" argued Nanny Piggins.

"No, it's not," argued the self-defense instructor.

"Do you want to bet?" challenged Nanny Piggins. "Defend yourself against this, then!" She hurled herself at his shins. It took her just three seconds to have him pressed into the mat in a total body lock.

"Where did you learn those techniques?" asked the self-defense instructor. "You could hurt someone."

"I know. They're good, aren't they?" agreed Nanny Piggins.

After they had sent the instructor home and Nanny Piggins had taught the group some really useful self-defense skills, the Neighborhood Watch held their meeting. Nanny Piggins and the children stayed, partly to be polite, and partly because there was a large tray of doughnuts on a side table to which anyone could help themselves.

"There were two more break-ins last night after our patrol finished," said Valerie. "We really need to get up more patrols. The burglars are just working out what times we aren't on the streets and striking then. Who can volunteer for more shifts?"

No one put their hands up.

"I need my rest," said one woman. "My grandchildren are visiting on the weekend. It always takes me two weeks to recover."

"And I can't take any more time away from my roses,"

said another man. "They get jealous if they think I am seeing other plants."

"And I can't," said a very wrinkly old man, "because I don't want to. And I'm too old to be doing things I don't want to do."

"Perhaps our new members would like to help?" said Valerie as she looked meaningfully at Nanny Piggins.

Samantha nudged her nanny, and Nanny Piggins looked up from the five jelly-filled doughnuts she was trying to fit into her mouth all at once.

"Mmmfff?" asked Nanny Piggins.

"We would really appreciate your help," said Valerie. "All you need to do is walk the streets with a flashlight and check on everyone's homes."

Nanny Piggins swallowed the doughnuts and spoke with as much dignity as a pig covered in jelly and doughnut crumbs can muster. "You're asking me to go around the neighborhood at night looking into people's homes with a flashlight?"

"Yes," said Valerie.

"Of course I'll do it!" said Nanny Piggins. "I love spying on people and violating their privacy. When do we start?"

"Tomorrow night," said Valerie.

It took some time for the children and Boris to persuade Nanny Piggins that her all-black outfit and camouflage paint were not necessary for performing a Neighborhood Watch patrol.

"The idea is that the burglars *do* see you and keep away," said Derrick.

"But if they see me, I'll lose the element of surprise when I attack," explained Nanny Piggins.

"You know you promised the Police Sergeant you would stop attacking people, regardless of the crimes against fashion you think they are committing," said Boris.

"I only said that so he would take off the handcuffs," mumbled Nanny Piggins. "All right, I'll change."

When Nanny Piggins emerged from her bedroom a few moments later, she was wearing her hot-pink wrestling leotard again. The children did not know what to say.

"There's nothing wrong with this outfit, is there?" challenged Nanny Piggins.

"Well, the burglars will certainly be able to see you coming," agreed Derrick.

"And when they do, they'll definitely stay away," added Michael.

"But you're not planning to do any actual wrestling tonight, are you?" asked Samantha. If her nanny was going to attack criminals, she would need to take along extra supplies of recuperative chocolate.

"No, I have no plans. But it is best to be prepared," said Nanny Piggins airily as she picked up her official Neighborhood Watch flashlight and set out with Boris and the children into the streets of Dulsford.

It turned out that Neighborhood Watch patrolling was nowhere near as glamorous as Nanny Piggins had hoped. In the first five minutes of their patrol, they encountered no jewel thieves, kidnappers, or pirates. And Nanny Piggins did not even have much fun spying on her neighbors. Word had gotten out that she had joined the Neighborhood Watch, so everyone in the local area had been sure to draw their curtains, lock their doors, and make certain all the roof tiles were securely attached to their roofs.

They did have some fun going through Mrs. McGill's rubbish bins and counting all the empty ice-cream containers. And Nanny Piggins had enjoyed catching Mr. Mahmood's cat, then kicking in his back door to return it to him. But on the whole, walking the streets in the middle of the night was a little dull. When Nanny Piggins had agreed to become involved in crime prevention, she had assumed there would be some crime to prevent. Fortunately, however, she did not have to wait much longer before a serious infringement came to her attention.

They were walking along a street when they began to hear a loud throbbing noise.

"What on earth is that noise?" asked Nanny Piggins.

"It's some sort of dreadful pulsing sound," said Boris.

"Perhaps an evil scientist is testing some kind of doomsday device somewhere in the neighborhood," suggested Nanny Piggins hopefully.

"No, I think it's just someone having a party. It's music," said Derrick.

"Music?!" exclaimed Nanny Piggins.

"Surely not!" exclaimed Boris.

"Music has melody and rhythm," said Nanny Piggins.

"And it sounds nice," added Boris.

"But that is just a dreadful droning noise," said Nanny Piggins.

"It's like a headache coming from the outside of your head," agreed Boris.

"A lot of people like music that sounds like that," explained Samantha.

"Really?" said a bewildered Nanny Piggins. "Well then, we'll just have to put a stop to that! Come along." Nanny Piggins marched purposefully in the direction of the party noise.

"Should we stop her?" asked Samantha.

"Do you think you could?" asked Michael.

So they all hurried after Nanny Piggins, not wanting to miss out on the scene that was sure to follow.

Nanny Piggins knocked loudly on the front door of the house emitting the "music" and then took a few steps back, ready to do a flying sidekick to smash her way in, when the door swung open.

"Hello," said the teenager who answered the door.

"I am Nanny Piggins of the Neighborhood Watch," said Nanny Piggins boldly (not in the least self-conscious that she was wearing a hot-pink wrestling leotard).

"Oh, sorry. Do you want us to turn down the music?" asked the youth.

"I do not!" said Nanny Piggins. "This is a party, isn't it?"

"Um...yes," admitted the teenager.

"Then it would be wrong to have quiet music," said Nanny Piggins. "No, on behalf of the Neighborhood Watch and music lovers everywhere, I am ordering you to play *better* music."

"But this song is number three on the dance charts," protested the teenager.

"Pish!" said Nanny Piggins. "Out of my way. I can see I shall have to deal with this personally." Nanny Piggins pushed past the teenager, entered the house, found the stereo, and removed the offending MP3 player. "Boris, find me some real music."

Boris took the device and flipped through the downloaded tracks. "They don't have any. It's all alternative dance music, indie rock, and that dreadful wailing music young women listen to when they've broken up with their boyfriends."

"This is more serious than I realized," said Nanny Piggins. "Derrick, fetch me the telephone." Nanny Piggins turned to address the crowd of partygoers. "Don't panic, people, we'll soon have this sorted out."

Within fifteen minutes, an Argentinean milonga band who owed Nanny Piggins a favor (she had helped them escape Argentina during the dictatorship by firing them into Bolivia with her cannon) had arrived and started playing tango music. Nanny Piggins then proceeded to teach all two hundred of the young partygoers how to really dance.

It ended up being the best party any of them had ever been to. Even the most sullen of the young people started to brighten up when they listened to actual good music, played well, by real musicians instead of a computer. They all danced until dawn, then ate the cupcakes Nanny Piggins baked them for breakfast, before the party broke up and everyone headed home (to get dressed for school).

So Nanny Piggins was tangoing down the street with Derrick while Boris carried Samantha and a very sleepy Michael when they turned the corner and spotted Valerie from the Neighborhood Watch standing outside their house, waiting for them.

"Good morning," called Nanny Piggins. "We had a

wonderful patrol last night. I didn't have to wrestle with anybody. Which just goes to show that wearing a hot-pink wrestling leotard can be preventive. The rest of the Neighborhood Watch should consider adopting them as their uniform."

But Valerie did not appear to be impressed. "While you were out on patrol last night, there were seven break-ins."

"But we didn't see anything," said Nanny Piggins.

"Were you out on the street looking for crime?" asked Valerie.

"Well, no, we went into a home to prevent crime against music," admitted Nanny Piggins.

"You neglected your duties," accused Valerie. "You let the neighborhood down."

"But they were playing really dreadful music," explained Nanny Piggins. "Surely that is a greater crime than someone stealing a few material goods?"

"They stole Mrs. Cuthbert's massaging footbath," said Valerie.

"No," gasped Nanny Piggins, Boris, and the still-conscious children (Michael was fast asleep).

"These thieves are heartless," said Nanny Piggins.

"I am officially throwing you out of the Neighborhood Watch," announced Valerie. "Hand in your flashlight." Valerie held out her hand expectantly.

"But—" protested Nanny Piggins.

"No buts," said Valerie.

"I left my flashlight at the party," said Nanny Piggins.

"Typical," said Valerie. She turned on her heel and stalked away.

The children and Boris held their breath waiting for Nanny Piggins's response. It was not as explosive as they were expecting. But that only made it more frightening.

"Tonight I shall get revenge," said Nanny Piggins. "Revenge on the burglars for daring to break into houses on the night of my patrol. And revenge against the Neighborhood Watch for daring to throw me out of their organization, which, I might add, I would never have even joined in the first place if I had not been plied with so many free jelly-filled doughnuts!"

That night Nanny Piggins again donned her all-black clothes and camouflage paint. She then paid a visit to

Mrs. Simpson, the elderly widow next door, and borrowed the horn from her gramophone.

"What are you going to use that for?" asked Derrick.

"You know how, in the olden days, deaf people used to use an ear horn to aid their hearing?" asked Nanny Piggins. "Well, I am going to use this as a nose horn so I can amplify my already extraordinary sense of smell to track down these naughty burglars."

"You're going to sniff the burglars out?" asked Michael.

"Precisely," said Nanny Piggins. "Come along; there's no time to lose."

So Nanny Piggins, Boris, and the children again took to the streets, this time following Nanny Piggins as she sniffed through the gramophone horn.

"Can you smell anything?" asked Boris.

"There is an odor of mischief coming from that direction," said Nanny Piggins, pointing toward the end of the street. She closed her eyes and continued sniffing, and the others followed her. They followed Nanny Piggins to the top of the street, around the corner, across the park, down an alley, over a footbridge, and onto another street.

"Stop!" said Nanny Piggins.

"What is it?" asked Derrick.

"Can't you smell it?" asked Nanny Piggins. "There is someone up on that roof at the end of the block, trying to climb down through the chimney."

"Santa?" asked Boris hopefully.

"No," said Nanny Piggins, sniffing again. "A burglar."

As the children squinted into the darkness, they could just make out the even darker shape of someone standing on a roof.

"Derrick, use that call box to telephone the police. Tell them I am about to make a citizen's arrest," said Nanny Piggins as she strode toward the house.

"But how?" asked Michael.

"You will be careful, won't you?" worried Samantha.

"Pish," said Nanny Piggins as she started to climb a nearby tree. "It's that burglar who is going to wish he was more careful."

"Are you going to drop on him when he walks past?" asked Michael. He enjoyed it when his nanny ambushed people. Particularly when it was the milkman. She was always attacking him whenever he left skim milk by mistake.

"No, I've got a better idea," said Nanny Piggins. "Boris, grab this branch I'm sitting on and pull it down to the ground."

"All right," said Boris. Being ten feet tall and weighing over one thousand pounds meant that pulling back a large tree branch was easy for him.

"Now, let go!" ordered Nanny Piggins.

"Are you sure?" asked Boris.

"Just do it!" said Nanny Piggins.

"Okay," said Boris, letting go of the branch so that it whipped back up and hurled Nanny Piggins high in the air.

"Wow!" exclaimed Michael.

"What have I done?!" exclaimed Boris.

"Hand me some chocolate before I faint!" exclaimed Samantha.

Nanny Piggins shot up into the night sky, over the gable of the roof, and came down with a crash right on top of the burglar. They immediately started wrestling. Fortunately Nanny Piggins had her hot-pink wrestling leotard on under her black clothing, because the burglar was surprisingly good. Someone had obviously taught him some first-rate techniques. But Nanny Piggins won easily when they both fell off the roof into a hydrangea bush and Nanny Piggins used her superior aerial ability to ensure that she landed on top.

"You're under citizen's arrest!" said Nanny Piggins.

"Urh," moaned the burglar.

"Hurrah!" said Boris and the children as they rushed forward to check that Nanny Piggins was all right.

"How dare you steal from a nice person's home," chided Nanny Piggins. "But, more importantly, how dare you humiliate me in front of the Neighborhood Watch by stealing on the night of my patrol." And with that, she pulled the ski mask off the burglar's face and then recoiled in shock.

"Valerie Darvas?!" exclaimed Nanny Piggins. For beneath the ski mask was, indeed, the captain of the Neighborhood Watch.

"You silly pig," ranted Valerie. "I've been getting away with robbing the houses in this neighborhood for years using the Neighborhood Watch as my cover. And now you've ruined everything. I only invited you to join because I thought a pig would be the perfect patsy for my schemes."

In the distance, they could hear the sound of a siren as the police approached.

"Well, I hope you've learned your lesson," said Boris. "Never ever cross a flying pig."

The police soon dragged Valerie away. The Police Sergeant was so grateful to Nanny Piggins for solving Valerie's one-woman crime wave (681 burglaries over a 23-year period) that he gave Nanny Piggins permission to make as many citizen's arrests for crimes against fashion as she liked for a whole week. (Nanny Piggins planned to go down to the school first thing on Monday and round up all the teachers.)

It turned out that the free flashlight given out by the Neighborhood Watch to all new members actually contained a secret satellite-tracking device, which was how Valerie knew exactly where each Neighborhood Watch patrol member was and where she could strike. If she had not been evil, Nanny Piggins would have almost admired her.

"Have you ever considered joining the police force and being trained to make arrests properly?" asked the Police Sergeant.

"Oh no," said Nanny Piggins. "It is much more fun to be an amateur who dabbles. If I was arresting criminal masterminds every night, it would get tedious eventually."

"And it wouldn't be fair to the criminals," added Boris. "They'd be in jail all the time."

And so Nanny Piggins, Boris, and the children celebrated by playing another game of Spotlight in the backyard. They could not use their Neighborhood Watch flashlight because it was now in police custody as evidence. But they did insist that Nanny Piggins wear her hot-pink leotard to give the rest of them a sporting chance of tagging her.

CHAPTER THREE

Nanny Piggins's B & B

oooh. Aaaaahhh. Hoorraaayyy!!!" cheered the bus passengers as Nanny Piggins demonstrated the difference between a triple somersault and a double cutaway with a twist.

Derrick, Samantha, Michael, and Boris clapped and cheered too. This was the wonderful thing about riding public transportation with Nanny Piggins. You only had to say something in passing like, "So what are the different tricks you can do on a trapeze?" and before you knew it she had borrowed two silk ties from a pair of businessmen and a sturdy umbrella from a retired librarian, and rigged up a swinging trapeze from the handrail along the roof of the bus.

Nanny Piggins was just swooping back and forth, building up momentum, getting ready to do a backflip with a half pike, when the bus driver stopped the bus, got out of his seat, and started walking down the aisle toward her.

"I'm afraid I'm going to have to ask you to leave the bus," said the bus driver.

"Aww," groaned all the other passengers.

Nanny Piggins leaped off the swing, did a perfect double-tuck backflip, and landed gracefully on the middle of the last row of seats.

"Why?" she asked.

"Yes, why?" chorused the passengers.

"I haven't been able to take on any new passengers for the last seven stops because no one is getting off. They are all enjoying watching your performance," explained the bus driver. "And if I don't drop off or pick up any passengers I'm going to get in trouble when I get back to the bus depot."

"Oh," said Nanny Piggins. Normally she liked to buck authority, but a bus driver was not much of a figure of power, and she did not want to get him in trouble. "All right, but why do you have to throw us off the bus? Couldn't we just sit in our seats like normal passengers?"

"That won't work. The other passengers still won't get off," said the bus driver, "because they'll all want to get your autograph and have their photos taken with you."

"Is this true?" Nanny Piggins asked the other bus passengers.

They all nodded. Nanny Piggins was by far the most fabulous person any of them had ever met on a bus, or anywhere else for that matter.

"All right, I'll get off," said Nanny Piggins, "but I want a full refund on our tickets. If we are going to walk home, we will have to spend our fares on lollipops to recover from the ordeal."

"Thank you. Thank you so much," gushed the bus driver as he rushed back to the front to return the money for six tickets. (Even though there were only five of them, the bus driver had made Nanny Piggins buy two tickets for Boris because he took up two bus seats, which is the reason why the bus driver had become frightened of Nanny Piggins in the first place. She had spent a full five minutes telling him off for being species-ist and insensitive to an otherwise athletic bear who just happened to have big bones.)

Anyway, that is how Nanny Piggins, Boris, and the children came to be walking home. It was not a long walk, but walks with Nanny Piggins always took longer than they were supposed to. She kept wanting to stop and look at things in people's gardens, and sometimes go right into people's houses to confront them about the things she had found. For example, she did not understand garden gnomes at all, so she was forever confronting the owners and demanding that they explain their affection for diminutive bearded men.

On this particular occasion, they had been walking for just a few minutes when a sign in someone's front garden caught Nanny Piggins's eye:

LAVENDER COTTAGE B & B

VACANCY AVAILABLE

Nanny Piggins had a flood of questions. "How is a cottage different from a house?" "Why is it called *Lavender* Cottage when it is clearly made out of brick?" "Are the bricks made of lavender?" "What is a B & B?" "Do two bees live there?" "Does that mean they sell honey?"

The children struggled to think of the answers.

"Um…it's called a cottage because *cottage* sounds nice," explained Samantha.

"And the owner is calling it 'Lavender' because it's got that tiny wilted lavender bush near the front door," added Derrick.

"And B & B means bed-and-breakfast," explained Michael.

"They're selling beds and breakfasts?" asked Nanny Piggins. "What a curious shop. Still, it makes sense. Breakfast in bed is one of my seven favorite meals of the day. Really, when you think about it, it's amazing more restaurants don't serve meals in bed. It's much better than eating at a table, because if you drop something it doesn't fall on the floor, so you don't have to wait until everyone is looking the other way to pick it up and eat it. You can just scoop it straight up off the bedding and put it back in your mouth."

"No, a B & B is not a restaurant or a shop," explained Derrick. "It's a type of hotel. You stay the night and breakfast is included in the price."

"Ooooh," said Nanny Piggins. She liked any business transaction where breakfast was included.

"And how much do they charge for this service?" Nanny Piggins assumed it could not be much. It was rude to ask a guest for money to stay in your home, and breakfast food was very inexpensive. She supposed the most you could reasonably charge would be one or two dollars.

"About one hundred dollars," said Derrick. (Mrs. Green had often taken the children away for the weekend and stayed in B & Bs before she had died, so he was quite the expert.)

"One hundred dollars!" exclaimed Nanny Piggins.

"More if it's really fancy," said Michael.

"More? How fancy could it possibly be?" asked Boris.

"That depends on how much potpourri they put in your room," said Samantha wisely.

"Hmm," said Nanny Piggins as she stared long and hard at the sign. She did not say any more on the whole walk home, although she did borrow a pen and do a lot of arithmetic on the back of Michael's shirt while muttering to herself things like: "We're going to be rich, rich! Rich, I say!!"

As soon as they walked in the front door, Nanny Piggins made an announcement. "Well, children, I've decided to open a bed–and–breakfast," she declared.

"Oh," said Derrick.

Samantha and Boris just burst into tears, and Michael ran forward and clutched his nanny in the biggest hug he could manage.

"We'll miss you," said Derrick, bravely sniffling and trying to stop the tears leaking out of his eyes.

"What are you talking about?" asked Nanny Piggins. "I'm not going anywhere to do it."

"You're not?" asked Samantha.

"No, I'm going to open my B & B right here in the house," explained Nanny Piggins.

"But what about Father?" asked Derrick. "He'll never allow that!"

"Pish! He won't notice," said Nanny Piggins. Mr. Green's ability to not notice even very large things (for example, a ten-foot-tall dancing bear living in his garden shed) was really quite extraordinary.

"But where will you put the guests?" asked Michael.

"We can put two in the spare room, and another two in your father's room," said Nanny Piggins.

"With Father?!" asked Samantha.

"Of course not. We want our guests to have a pleasant time. No, I'll make a place for Mr. Green on the floor of the broom closet," said Nanny Piggins.

"But what will you tell Father when he asks why?" asked Derrick.

"What I always tell him," said Nanny Piggins. "To stop asking questions and do as he's told."

And so Nanny Piggins and the children set to work refurbishing the Green house. It did not take long because Nanny Piggins had a knack for interior decorating. They started by going to Mr. Green's room and throwing out all his personal possessions (a broken comb, a jar of hair grease, and a book about tax law); they then moved on to painting the four walls with a giant mural of a flying pig dazzling a big top full of circus-goers. This completely transformed his bedroom from a dowdy, unpleasant place that smelled slightly of dirty socks into a glamorous boudoir where people could actually enjoy spending time.

Next, Nanny Piggins turned her talents to the living

room. It was full of old, musty furniture that Mr. Green's great-grandmother had foolishly left unattended in her locked garage. The furniture had been hideous when it was brand-new back in the nineteenth century, so now it was both hideous and old. Obviously something radical needed to be done.

Nanny Piggins decided to pay a visit to the retired Army Colonel who lived around the corner (and was deeply in love with her) and borrow some of his old parachutes from when he was a paratrooper. She then got Boris to drape the huge sheets of silk down from the ceiling, which made the room look like an indoor tent. Then she covered all the furniture with faux leopard-print velvet, which gave the house an exotic safari feel.

Finally, Nanny Piggins dramatically improved the appearance of the front of the house by putting up a huge sign:

NANNY PIGGINS'S B & B & S & C & C & MC
VACANCY AVAILABLE

"What does B-and-B-and-S-and-C-and-C-and-MC stand for?" asked Michael curiously.

"Bed-and-Breakfast-and-Show-and-Cake-and-Chocolate-and-More Chocolate," explained Nanny Piggins. "If I'm going to charge money, I thought I should throw in a few extra things to make it good value."

"That's brilliant," said Derrick.

"Why would anyone want to stay anywhere else?" agreed Boris.

"But surely Father will notice the sign," worried Samantha. It was very large, and Nanny Piggins had used every color of paint in her paint box.

"I doubt it," said Nanny Piggins confidently. "Now we're all set up. We just have to sit back and wait for our first guest."

Nanny Piggins's B & B & S & C & C & MC was soon inundated with enquiries. There was a dental convention in town, and since dentists lead such dull lives, the idea of staying somewhere that offered a show—plus cake, plus chocolate, plus more chocolate—really appealed to them. (When you are a dentist, you can never really enjoy eating chocolate in your hometown in case one of your patients spots you, which is why dentists always love to go away to conventions, so they can binge on sugary foods.)

By the end of the week, the B & B & S & C & C & MC was so full of visitors Nanny Piggins herself had to move in with Samantha to make another room available. And Nanny Piggins turned Mr. Green out of his office saying that he could not get in there for two weeks because there was a uranium deposit under the floor and he had to wait until it reached its half-life. (Nanny Piggins was sure that when it came to anything involving the exponential decay of radioactive material, Mr. Green, like most people, would be too proud to admit that he did not have a clue what she was talking about.)

Amazingly, Mr. Green did not notice the sign on his front lawn, the parachutes in his living room, the cabaret show being performed in the kitchen every night, nor the seven extra people sitting around the breakfast table every morning (eating the most spectacular breakfast they had ever had in their lives) until they had been there for three days. And then he was too embarrassed to say something in front of strangers, when they were clearly such upright respectable citizens because their teeth were so shiny.

Instead he followed Nanny Piggins out to the kitchen as she was taking away the plates (to fetch fifth helpings of triple-chocolate-fudge pancakes for everybody).

"Um, Nanny Piggins," began Mr. Green. "Perhaps you could tell me. Who are those, er...people sitting around the breakfast table?"

"Mr. Green, shame on you," scolded Nanny Piggins.

"What have I done?" asked Mr. Green as he went bright red in the face. (He had done so many shameful things he was wondering which one Nanny Piggins was referring to. Mr. Green just hoped she did not know about the hedge fund he had set up using the money Mrs. Green had left in her will for the children's education. Actually Nanny Piggins did know, but she thought a *hedge fund* was when someone put aside money to grow a row of bushes in the garden, so she was yet to appreciate the full wickedness of Mr. Green's actions.)

"Don't you recognize them?" asked Nanny Piggins. "They are your cousins. They are paying you a visit."

"Well, throw them out!" exclaimed Mr. Green, totally aghast. "I don't want relatives staying in my home!" As far as Mr. Green was concerned, it was bad enough he had to give house space to his children.

"All right, if you insist," said Nanny Piggins, turning back toward the dining room.

"I insist," insisted Mr. Green.

"It's just a shame when they're so rich," said Nanny Piggins.

"What did you say?" asked Mr. Green as he leaped with surprising agility to block Nanny Piggins's path. (Talk of money always brought out Mr. Green's athletic side.)

"They're your rich cousins," replied Nanny Piggins. "The ones who are thinking about leaving you all that money in their wills."

"Really?" asked Mr. Green. "Just how rich are they?"

"Very, very," said Nanny Piggins. "You see that woman over there?" Nanny Piggins pushed the door open a crack and pointed to one of the dentists. "The one eating strawberry jam out of the jar with her finger? Well, she told me she is so rich she never has to wear a pair of socks twice. When she takes them off, she throws them away. And the next day she puts on some brand-new ones."

"The decadence!" gasped Mr. Green. He personally wore every single one of his socks for years and years until they totally disintegrated and became just tangles of thread at the bottom of his shoes.

"Still, if they don't leave it to you, I'm sure all their money will go to another worthy cause," said Nanny Piggins. "Perhaps the Cat Protection Society."

"Cats!" screamed Mr. Green.

"Or the Home for Retired Circus Pigs," continued Nanny Piggins.

"Pigs!" squealed Mr. Green, before struggling to compose himself. "Um, Nanny Piggins, I think after all, since family is so important, we really must be hospitable to our cousins. Here, let me carry that food out to them. Don't stint on the cream. We must keep them happy."

And so, not only did Mr. Green fail to notice that his nanny was running a bed-and-breakfast in his very own house, he also allowed himself to be tricked into becoming the unpaid bellboy, waiter, and errand runner, scurrying around after all the guests and fulfilling their every wish.

"Where do you find such good staff?" asked one of the dentists, as Mr. Green lay rose petals at her feet to welcome her home after a long day at the convention.

"The secret is the training," admitted Nanny Piggins truthfully. "You have to be very strict. And if they're naughty, don't be afraid to give them a little smack on the nose with a rolled-up newspaper."

Things were going very well. The house was full of guests every night, and Nanny Piggins had made many, many hundreds of dollars. Admittedly, she had not saved any of it. Nanny Piggins believed in investing money. So she invested all the profits into the breakfasts. And that investment paid dividends.

The breakfasts Nanny Piggins served were by far the most amazing breakfasts eaten anywhere in the world ever. She had waffles flown in from Belgium every morning; the finest chocolatiers in Switzerland were custom-making a special breakfast chocolate to Nanny Piggins's specifications (it was a chocolate that contained extra chocolate); and, of course, Nanny Piggins baked her own mouthwateringly good cakes. At the end of the meal, some of the dentists actually wept because the food was so good (and because they knew once the conference was over, they would have to go back home to their sugarless gum and gargling with fluoride mouthwash).

Even Mr. Green was enjoying himself. Sometimes after he had carried a particularly heavy suitcase up three flights of stairs, or helped an overweight guest cut his toenails, or run into town to fetch an important chocolate delivery, one of the "cousins" would press a quarter into his hand as a thank-you. Mr. Green loved getting tips. He would rush to his broom closet and hoard it carefully in an old jar of silver polish.

All in all, Nanny Piggins's B & B & S & C & C & MC could not have been a happier place. Then one day, an important-looking envelope arrived in the mail. (You are probably wondering how an envelope can look important. Well, this one did. It was made of heavy cream-colored paper, the type that can give you a nasty paper cut if you try to open it by sticking your finger in the edge.) And inside there was a card that read: YOUR B & B HAS BEEN BROUGHT TO OUR ATTENTION AS BEING OF THE SUPERIOR VARIETY. A CRITIC WILL VISIT YOU SHORTLY TO ASSESS YOUR ESTABLISH-MENT FOR INCLUSION IN THE *MAXWELLIAN GUIDE*.

"You're going to be reviewed by the *Maxwellian Guide!*" gasped Boris. "That's wonderful." (Boris knew all about Maxwellian guidebooks. His performance of *Swan Lake* had once been reviewed by a Maxwellian critic who said, "Boris the Bear's portrayal of a dying swan was so beautiful it made me want to join Greenpeace and fight for swans' rights.")

"It is?" asked Nanny Piggins. She had never heard of Maxwellian guides before.

"If you get five Maxwellian stars, the B & B will be packed every night," explained Boris.

"It is already packed every night," said Nanny Piggins.

"Yes, but it will be packed with a different type of people—rich people. You will be able to charge them more," said Boris.

"More than a hundred dollars a night?!" exclaimed Nanny Piggins, struggling to wrap her mind around the concept. "What do you mean? One hundred dollars and fifty cents?"

"No, more than that. If you have five Maxwellian stars, you could charge one hundred and twenty dollars!" declared Boris.

Nanny Piggins had to sit down and dab her forehead. "But that is so much money. I wouldn't dare."

"People wouldn't mind," Derrick assured her.

"I heard one of the dentists say he would sell his house just for one of your chocolate éclairs," said Michael.

"And think what you could do with all that money," said Samantha.

"You could buy another shed for the garden and move Father out of the house entirely," suggested Michael.

"Or you could buy that catapult you've had your eye on," suggested Derrick.

"Or you could buy more chocolate," said Boris, because he knew his sister best, so he knew which would be the most convincing argument.

"All right, let's do it. Let's impress that critic," decided Nanny Piggins.

"How?" asked Samantha.

"Well, everything already looks fabulous. And I don't think I could do anything to improve the breakfasts, short of inventing a new element for the periodic table and calling it chocolatonium," said Nanny Piggins. "Really there is only one blemish on Nanny Piggins's B & B."

"What is it?" asked the children.

Michael quickly tried to rub off the chocolate smear behind his ear in case that was the blemish she was referring to. But it was not.

"Your father," said Nanny Piggins. "I think we will have to hide him."

"You could put a lampshade on his head," suggested Boris.

"That works when *you* do it because you are a ballet dancer, so you can make your body look like a lamp stand," said Nanny Piggins. "But I doubt Mr. Green has the same ability."

"You could lock him in the broom closet," suggested Derrick.

"Hmm, locking people in closets is very heavily frowned on by social services," said Nanny Piggins.

"It's just a shame that technically this is Father's house," said Michael.

"I know. Never mind, we'll just have to hope for the best," decided Nanny Piggins. "If the critic does meet your father, I can always explain that I hired him as a bellboy as part of a program to help keep lunatics off the streets."

The next morning, Nanny Piggins and the children stood in the front hallway waiting for the arrival of the critic.

"How will we know who he is when he arrives?" asked Michael.

"Hopefully he'll tell us," said Nanny Piggins. "Otherwise we'll just have to search all the guests' luggage until we find him."

But they need not have worried. It became immediately apparent who Wolfgang Van Der Porten was as soon as he got out of his limousine. Nanny Piggins had never seen a man hold his nose so high in the air without the aid of standing on stilts. He did not greet his welcoming party, even though Nanny Piggins stepped forward and held out her trotter. He merely shrugged his coat off his shoulders (so it fell to the floor, the first bad mark for Nanny Piggins's B & B—no one had leaped forward to catch it), took out a little notepad, and started scribbling down criticisms.

"I see your entrance has a floor and a ceiling. How predictable," the critic said dismissively before sailing into the living room. "An indoor tent! How last autumn of you."

"Would you like some chocolate?" offered Nanny Piggins, rushing forward with a plate of Nanny Piggins's Special Breakfast Chocolate (the most welcoming gesture she knew).

"Yuck! I can't stand the stuff," said the critic, turning his nose up even higher. "Chocolate rots your teeth, clouds the mind, and clogs the bowels. Take it away."

Nanny Piggins did not take the chocolate away. She ate it to get over the shock of meeting someone who did not like chocolate.

"I don't think he's going to like your breakfast, then," whispered Michael.

The critic continued to wander about the house writing down more criticisms—"vertical walls—what a cliché," "faucets you have to turn on with your hands—how rustic," and "no gym, but a twenty-four-hour all-you-can-eat cake buffet—so unhealthy."

"What a simply dreadful man," muttered Nanny Piggins. "He could get a job in the circus. People would pay to come and stare at him. I don't think I've ever met anyone so horrible. Except of course your—"

At that exact moment Mr. Green entered the room, spotted the critic, and immediately started groveling. "Ah, cousin, so good to see you!"

"Cousin? What a peculiar greeting," said the critic.

"We're all family here," said Mr. Green, bowing so low his nose actually touched the carpet. "Is there anything I can do for you? Rub your feet? Hand-wash your underwear? Run into town to fetch you anything, anything at all?"

"Really? Anything, you say? Well, what if I said I wanted a sack full of lead ball bearings?" asked the critic.

"Right away," said Mr. Green, after which he dashed out of the house.

"Just as I thought. Staff making promises they can't fulfill," criticized the critic as he continued to scrawl in his notepad.

But half an hour later, the critic was astonished to see Mr. Green sweating his way back up the street carrying a heavy sack full of lead.

"Extraordinary," exclaimed the critic.

"Anything for a rich...I mean, a *dear* cousin," panted Mr. Green.

"This is some kind of stunt, isn't it?" said the critic. "Well, we'll just see how servile your service really is. Do five hundred jumping jacks."

"Of course," agreed Mr. Green as he launched into the horrible exercise. By the time he finished, Mr. Green had gone purple in the face, but he continued to smile at the man he thought was his rich cousin. The critic just stared at him. In his thirty years of reviewing hotels, he had never met anyone so obsequiously obedient.

Nanny Piggins and the children watched in enthralled wonder, waiting to see what the critic would make Mr. Green do next.

"Fetch me a garden salad," demanded the critic.

"Er...right away," said Mr. Green, disappearing into the kitchen.

"This ought to be good," said Nanny Piggins. "I bet your father has no idea what a garden salad is." Nanny Piggins did not know herself, but she was sure a meal that contained the words *garden* and *salad* could not be good.

Mr. Green rushed back a few moments later with a large bowl of grass clippings. Nanny Piggins had been right. Mr. Green knew nothing about preparing any type of meal, so he had simply run out into the garden and grabbed a handful of the first green thing he saw. Luckily for Mr. Green, however, a pure grass garden salad was all the rage in Paris that week, so the critic could not have been more impressed.

"Well, Nanny Piggins, your decor is hideous, the

A pure grass garden salad was all the rage in Paris that week, so the critic could not have been more impressed.

pervasive stench of chocolate throughout every room is nauseating, and I am pretty sure I saw a ten-foot-tall bear roaming about in the garden. But I have to say, this member of your staff is so utterly grovelingly obliging—I love it. I am going to give your B & B five stars," declared the critic.

"Hooray!" cheered Nanny Piggins and the children.

"Thanks to the *Maxwellian Guide*, your B & B will soon be filled with the richest, most exclusive international travelers," said the critic. "People just like me."

"What?" said Nanny Piggins.

"I shall ensure that all my friends and colleagues, all the people who share my attitudes and values, will visit here," explained the critic.

It took Nanny Piggins exactly two minutes and seven seconds to throw the critic out (she dragged him to the front door by his ear and pushed him down the front steps), politely ask the remaining dentists to leave, return the parachutes to the retired colonel around the corner, and close down her B & B forever.

"That was a near miss," said Nanny Piggins as she, Boris, and the children sat around the kitchen table eating chocolate to recover from their ordeal. "Money is lovely. And the chocolate you can buy with money is even lovelier. But it is not worth sacrificing your principles. And I make it a point of principle to never let anyone even more unbearable than your father stay in this house."

The children would have voiced their agreement if their mouths had not been so very full of Nanny Piggins's Special Breakfast Chocolate.

CHAPTER FOUR

Nanny Piggins Treads the Boards

"How was school today?" asked Nanny Piggins as Derrick, Samantha, and Michael got off the bus.

"Excellent!" exclaimed Michael. "Suzanne Foo brought in a big black spider and it ran up the librarian's leg."

"Really? She must have trained it well." Nanny Piggins approved.

"And gym was canceled because it rained!" said Samantha delightedly.

"What luck!" agreed Nanny Piggins. "What about you, Derrick? Did you have a good day?"

"All right, I suppose," said Derrick, "except Mr. Sriskandaraja caught me duct-taping Barry Nichols's leg to a table. Now as punishment I've got to write a one-thousand-word essay on the great Italian explorer Marco Polo."

"But that's wonderful news!" exclaimed Nanny Piggins.

"It is?" asked Derrick.

"Of course. Although it does mean you'll all have to take tomorrow off school," Nanny Piggins added.

"It does?" asked all three Green children.

"Absolutely, because Derrick will need to do research," explained Nanny Piggins. "And if he is going to research Marco Polo, he should obviously start by going down to the public swimming pool and playing the game Marco Polo. Because, as I'm sure all scholars would agree, while discovering China and introducing pasta to Europe were important, the invention of the game Marco Polo was by far his greatest achievement."

And so the next day, Nanny Piggins left a message on Headmaster Pimplestock's answering machine explaining that Derrick, Samantha, and Michael could not go to school because the World Health Organization had asked them to find a cure for hiccups. (Even though, really, Nanny Piggins already knew the cure—eat chocolate.) Then they all went to the pool.

Now, being blindfolded and chasing your friends while you scream "Marco!" and they scream "Polo!" is a lovely way to enjoy a backyard pool. But it is ten times more fun in a fifty-meter, eight-lane public pool. Especially once Nanny Piggins had persuaded all the people swimming up and down in the lanes to stop what they were doing and join the game. (It did not take much persuading—people swimming up and down in lanes are never having a wonderful time.)

Pretty soon there were forty-one adults of varying ages, as well as a pig (Nanny Piggins), a ten-foot-tall bear (Boris), and the three Green children playing the best and most raucous game of Marco Polo ever. The lifeguard tried to put a stop to it, even though they were not breaking any rules, because lifeguards instinctively feel they have to put a stop to anything noisy or fun. But Nanny Piggins offered him a slice of cake (a bit damp from falling in the pool), complimented him on his whistle, and flirted with him until the lifeguard was so charmed he was soon begging to be Marco in the next round.

Four hours later, after they were finally thrown out of the pool when the manager came out of his office and burst into tears upon seeing a giant bear demonstrating water aerobics,[1] Nanny Piggins, Boris, and the children were feeling very exhilarated as they walked home eating ice-cream cones. That was until the most dreadful and unexpected thing happened.

They bumped into Mr. Green, literally.

One moment they were all walking along watching a particularly exciting helicopter fly overhead, and the next moment they heard a *thump*, then a *thud*, then an *oomph*. And when they looked down they saw Mr. Green sprawled on the sidewalk having walked straight into, and bounced straight off of, Boris. Boris immediately hid

---

[1]The manager burst into tears because bears are hairy, and he was the one who had to clean the pool filter.

behind a telephone pole so he could remain incognito. But Nanny Piggins and the children peered down at Mr. Green, wondering what he was doing walking along a street in broad daylight.

Mr. Green normally went to the office before sunup and came home very late at night. (In fact, his avoidance of daylight was so complete that Nanny Piggins had been convinced he was a vampire for the first three months she had known him. The only thing that finally persuaded her that Mr. Green was not a vampire was that he was too boring to be a bloodsucking creature of the night.)

"What are you doing here?" demanded Nanny Piggins.

"I might ask the same of you," said Mr. Green, picking himself up, dusting himself off, and checking over his shoulder to make sure nobody could see him talking to a pig. "Shouldn't the children be in school?"

"They were given the day off because all the teachers had toothaches," fabricated Nanny Piggins.

"Really?" asked Mr. Green.

"Oh yes, teachers are forever secretly gobbling lollipops under their desks. That is why they have such terrible tempers—too much sugar in their diet," said Nanny Piggins. She did not believe for a moment that it was possible for anyone to have too much sugar in their diet, but she rightly guessed that Mr. Green would not be listening to her.

"I'll be on my way, then," said Mr. Green.

"Where?" asked Nanny Piggins, as she stepped in front of Mr. Green to block his path.

"It's none of your business where I'm going," said Mr. Green gruffly, which really was a very silly thing to say, because nothing makes a person more intrigued than being told that something is not their business.

"You really shouldn't have said that," said Samantha with a sigh as she noted a gleam appearing in her nanny's eye.

"Just tell Nanny Piggins what you're doing, Father," suggested Michael. "You know it will be a lot easier in the long run."

But whatever Mr. Green was up to was clearly embarrassing because his face turned red, he looked furtively over his shoulder, then he blustered, "If you'll be so kind...just go home...that is an order." And with this he flipped up his collar to hide his face and scurried away.

"What do you think he's up to?" asked Derrick.

"Perhaps he's fallen in with criminals," suggested Michael hopefully.

"Or he's been fired from his job for being boring," suggested Samantha realistically.

"Or he's rushing down to the pool having heard that there was a really excellent game of Marco Polo going on there," suggested Boris.

"Or all three! He's probably been fired for falling in with criminals who want to play Marco Polo," said Nanny Piggins as she watched Mr. Green scurry away in the distance. "We should follow him just to find out for sure."

"Wouldn't that be an invasion of Father's privacy?" asked Derrick.

"Oh yes," said Nanny Piggins, "but fathers shouldn't have privacy. It's part of being a normal parent to have no personal time, property, or space. Come on, let's follow him."

The children did not need to be persuaded. They were burning with curiosity. And it seemed silly to go to school now when half the day was already over. So they all took off running after Mr. Green before he disappeared into the distance.

Fortunately Mr. Green was not an observant man, so he did not notice he was being followed by his own children, their nanny, and a giant dancing bear. Plus Nanny Piggins was very good at "tailing a perp" (which is police talk for following a criminal), having read so many detective novels. She knew the trick was that as soon as the person you are following starts to turn around, you have to freeze in the middle of what you are doing and pretend to be a lost foreign tourist by having a loud conversation about street signs in German. This ruse worked well. So Nanny Piggins, Boris, and the children were only a few yards behind Mr. Green when they saw him disappear through the side door of the most disreputable type of building imaginable—a theater.

"A theater!" exclaimed Nanny Piggins. "What on earth could he be doing in there?"

"Buying theater tickets?" suggested Samantha.

"When have you ever known your father to voluntarily spend money on something pleasurable?" asked Nanny Piggins.

"True," conceded Samantha.

Just then, something caught Michael's eye. "Hey, look at that sign!"

They all looked up at a sign stuck to the back of the stage door:

OPEN AUDITION FOR
THE AMATEUR THEATER SOCIETY'S PRODUCTION OF
SHAKESPEARE'S *HAMLET*
ALL WELCOME

Nanny Piggins, Boris, and the children were shocked. Nanny Piggins even considered fainting, but then thought better of it, because the sidewalk did not look clean, and she was wearing an especially lovely outfit.

"Your father is auditioning for a play!" exclaimed Nanny Piggins.

"And he's taking time off work to do it!" marveled Derrick.

"Remind me that when he comes home, I need to bite his leg," said Nanny Piggins.

"Why?" asked Samantha.

"This is so out of character, I had better check that

he's not been kidnapped and replaced with a robot clone," explained Nanny Piggins.

"What are we going to do?" asked Michael. "Father obviously doesn't want us here."

"You're right. Which is why we must go in and watch. If your father is going to embarrass himself, it is important there are a lot of witnesses," said Nanny Piggins. "Humiliation doesn't really count unless there are lots of people to constantly remind you about it for years and years to come."

So Nanny Piggins, Boris, and the children let themselves into the theater and found seats up toward the back in the dark where they could watch the auditions. It soon became apparent why Mr. Green was auditioning. The director of the production and president of the Amateur Theater Society was a very attractive widow named Mrs. Fortescue-Brown, and Mr. Green was clearly smitten with her.

"A funny thing happened this morning at the office, Mrs. Fortescue-Brown," began Mr. Green, smirking and trying to look handsome. "I asked my clerk to fetch me volume thirteen of the taxation code, and he brought me volume seven, because he can't read roman numerals! Ha. Ha-ha." Mr. Green had to laugh at the end of his own joke because nobody else did, because it was not really a joke. (Mistaking sentences for jokes is a very common mistake made by aspiring comedians.)

"That's lovely, Mr. Green," said Mrs. Fortescue-Brown. "Now be a dear and sit over there until it is your turn to try out."

Nanny Piggins was right about the auditions being enormously entertaining. This was partly because she had hot-wired the popcorn machine and they were having a lovely time throwing popcorn at Boris and watching him leap up and pirouette in midair before catching them in his mouth. And partly because all the people auditioning were so awful.

Some were so shy they spoke in a whisper and could not be heard. Some were so bold they yelled every line. And not one of them could act. There is a real trick to saying every word as though you have absolutely no idea what it means, and every one of these amateurs had exactly that knack. As a professional circus performer, Nanny Piggins never realized that some people could be so bad at dazzling a crowd.

"What I don't understand is that if they are so talentless at acting, why didn't they bring a cannon?" asked Nanny Piggins. "Then at least they could finish with a bang."

Finally it was Mr. Green's turn. He walked up onstage and stood in front of the assembled crowd. Nanny Piggins, Boris, and the children held their breath in anticipation, wondering just how bad Mr. Green would be. Or perhaps he would surprise them and actually be good?

They soon found out as Mr. Green started to recite, "To be, or not to be..."

Nanny Piggins, Boris, and the children instantly burst out laughing. Mr. Green was even more awful than they had expected. There was something about the way his jowls quivered and his top lip sweated when he was trying to sound impressive that really was very funny.

"...That is the question. Whether it is..." continued Mr. Green.

"Make him stop!" called Boris. Not to be mean, but for health reasons, because he was laughing so hard he thought he was going to crack a rib.

Mr. Green did not notice. He was so absorbed in

"Make him stop!" called Boris.

trying to sound important, he would not have noticed if a steamroller had driven through the theater. But Mrs. Fortescue-Brown was more observant. She shot to her feet, turned around, and proceeded to scold Nanny Piggins and the children. (Boris quickly hid behind a plaster replica statue of the Venus de Milo.)

"Look here," said Mrs. Fortescue-Brown. "It's not as easy as it looks, saying all those lines. If you're so smart, why don't you come down here and give it a try?"

Nanny Piggins hopped out of her seat.

"All right, I will," she said. She ran down to the front of the theater and leaped onto the stage. Mr. Green dropped his copy of the play and hurried away. He did not want to be known to have a working relationship with a pig. Nanny Piggins scooped up the text and found the right page.

"When you're ready," said Mrs. Fortescue-Brown.

"I'm always ready," said Nanny Piggins.

"Then begin," said Mrs. Fortescue-Brown.

Nanny Piggins did not need to be told twice. She immediately launched into Hamlet's famous speech.

Now reader, this is a hard part for me as an author,

because this is where I have to describe Nanny Piggins's performance. And how do you describe perfection? Suffice it to say that never before, in the four hundred years since *Hamlet* was written, have those words been spoken so beautifully. Being such a gifted performer, Nanny Piggins instantly had the whole audience enthralled—she made them think, she made them laugh, she made them cry, she made them want to call their mothers as soon as they got home—so that when Nanny Piggins uttered the last syllable, everyone in the theater (except Mr. Green) leaped to their feet and burst into applause.

"That was brilliant, breathtaking, awesome!" gushed Mrs. Fortescue-Brown as she pumped Nanny Piggins's trotter up and down and slapped her on the back.

"I know," said Nanny Piggins truthfully.

"You have to accept the lead role," said Mrs. Fortescue-Brown. "We need you to play Hamlet."

"What?!" exploded Mr. Green. "But she's a woman!"

"So?" said Mrs. Fortescue-Brown. "Men played women all the time in Shakespeare's day."

"And she's a...she's a..." (Mr. Green found it hard to say the following words.) "She's a pig!" he hissed.

"The play is called 'Ham-let,'" said Nanny Piggins. "I assumed it was about a pig. It's not called Man-let, is it?"

"Good point," said Mrs. Fortescue-Brown, turning to her assistant. "Make a note to mention that in all the publicity."

So Nanny Piggins, the children, and Mr. Green returned home. Mr. Green sulked the whole way because he had only been given the part of second tree from the left (and first tree from the left was being played by a sheet of cardboard).

As soon as they got home, Mr. Green locked himself in his study so he could work on the portrayal of his character. He had a lot of important creative decisions to make—oak or cedar? Evergreen or deciduous? It would take hours.

Meanwhile Nanny Piggins went into the living room and found a comfortable seat so she could begin reading *Hamlet*.

Before we go on, I should explain something—Nanny Piggins had worked in the circus for many years, where she had performed in five shows a night, seven nights a week. As a result, she never had the opportunity to attend the theater herself, which meant she had never seen any of Shakespeare's plays. Obviously she knew parts of Hamlet's famous soliloquies from watching television, because her favorite character, Bethany on *The Young and the Irritable*, had once stolen the identity of an English professor. But when Nanny Piggins began reading *Hamlet*, she was utterly shocked.

"But this play is not written in English!" Nanny Piggins exclaimed in horror. "There's all these strange words like 'forsooth,' 'egad,' and 'prithee' written through it. Is that from some Polynesian dialect I'm not familiar with?"

"No, it's English," Samantha assured her. "It's the type of English everyone spoke four hundred years ago when Shakespeare wrote the play."

"Really?" said Nanny Piggins, not believing that anybody would actually talk such gobbledygook just because they had been alive four centuries ago.

Nanny Piggins's disapproval did not end there. She

had only been reading a few more minutes when she became so appalled, she leaped to her feet and threw the play on the floor in disgust.

"Piffle!" exclaimed Nanny Piggins, wanting to say something much worse.

"What's wrong?" asked Derrick.

"Hamlet," declared Nanny Piggins, "is a very, very bad man."

"What has he done?" asked Michael curiously.

"He was rude to his mother!" said Nanny Piggins disapprovingly.

The children gasped. They knew Nanny Piggins did not approve of young men being rude to their mothers.

"Just because he is the Prince of Denmark does not give him the right to speak to her that way," ranted Nanny Piggins. She then picked up the play and kept reading, wanting to find out if his mother would get fed up and bite Hamlet's leg.

But Nanny Piggins was soon distracted by other fundamental faults in Shakespeare's great work. "Tsk, tsk, tsk," said Nanny Piggins as she avidly read on.

"What is it?" asked Derrick.

"This play is very violent," said Nanny Piggins.

"You like rough-and-tumble," Michael reminded her.

"Of course, everyone enjoys a good sword fight," said Nanny Piggins. "But there are so *many* sword fights. This Shakespeare fellow needs a good editor. Someone to tell him to swap one or two of these sword fights for pie fights. That would be a lot more fun. And you would lose less characters that way."

As Nanny Piggins approached the end of *Hamlet*, tears began to trickle down her face, then she started to sob, and finally she began to wail loudly.

"What's wrong?" worried Boris, rushing to give his sister a big hug.

"It's the ending," said Nanny Piggins. "It's so awful."

"How awful?" asked Derrick.

"It's worse than the episode of *The Young and the Irritable* where Bethany and Rock get married on that Caribbean cruise ship with the bomb in the engine room."

The others were astonished.

"How can anything be worse than episode 3,791 of *TYATI*?" asked Samantha. "That is the saddest program on television ever."

"The producers had to bring six characters back from the dead because they had so many complaints from viewers," added Derrick.

"*Hamlet* is worse than that," said Nanny Piggins definitively as she finished the last page of the play and closed the book. "Well, that settled it. If I am going to star in this production, I will just have to rewrite the play."

"Can you do that?" asked Samantha. From everything Samantha's English teacher had said, Samantha had come to believe that the words of Shakespeare were objects of sacred art—like Leonardo da Vinci's paintings, Michelangelo's sculptures, or Jamie Oliver's cookbooks. They were something that should be in a museum and only be viewed from behind a velvet rope.

"Of course I can," said Nanny Piggins. "I have a pen, don't I? And I'm only going to improve it. I'm sure if Shakespeare were alive today he would be grateful for my help."

And so Nanny Piggins got out a pen and twenty pounds of chocolate (for inspiration) and set to work improving *Hamlet*. She wrote all afternoon, all night, and into the next morning. The children even went to school so Nanny Piggins could have time to write (and Derrick could present his Marco Polo research). When they returned home, they found their exhausted nanny slumped on the sofa fast asleep, clutching a highly annotated copy of *Hamlet*.

.... ★ ★ ★ ....

Later that day, when they arrived at the first rehearsal, things did not go quite as Nanny Piggins had imagined. Nanny Piggins had expected Mrs. Fortescue-Brown to be eternally grateful when she presented her new, improved version of *Hamlet*. But instead, Mrs. Fortescue-Brown immediately quit in disgust and stormed off in a huff because she expected everyone from the cast to rush after her and beg her to come back (which just goes to show how silly some people's expectations can be).

The problem was, the cast soon read Nanny Piggins's *Hamlet* and agreed it was much better, although their judgment may have been compromised. Nanny Piggins had brought along two dozen large chocolate cakes, whereas Mrs. Fortescue-Brown had only brought a small bowl of carrot sticks. It was obvious who had the upper hand. Nanny Piggins was immediately elected the new director.

In the weeks that followed, Nanny Piggins, Boris, and the children had a wonderful time rehearsing *Hamlet* with the Amateur Theater Society. The children learned so much, such as how to look even more beautiful than usual with the aid of half a million dollars' worth of professional lighting; how to not really kill each other when having a pretend sword fight; and how to tell off your uncle if you think he's poured poison in your father's ear.

So when Mr. Sriskandaraja caught Derrick climbing out of a window during a particularly boring poetry lesson and gave him the punishment of writing an essay on the themes of *Hamlet*, he was surprised to get back a brilliantly insightful essay revealing Derrick's subtle and complex understanding of the psychoanalytical issues in the Bard's great work.

The big night of the first performance soon arrived.

"Are you nervous, Nanny Piggins?" asked Samantha.

"Oh no," said Nanny Piggins. "I just feel bad for all the other playwrights who are going to be put to shame as soon as the public sees my masterpiece."

"Don't you mean Shakespeare's masterpiece?" reminded Michael.

"I suppose he had something to do with it," conceded Nanny Piggins begrudgingly. "I have kept some of his original character names, but really, the more I think about his version, the more I wonder how he ever got away with it."

The auditorium was jam-packed. Even all the standing room at the back of the theater was sold out. Mrs. Fortescue-Brown was there with all her friends, ready to hate the play and enjoy complaining about it at length. All the local Shakespeare lovers had arrived (both of them). All the pig fans were there (a surprisingly large group), who were interested to see how a pig would interpret the role. And finally there were the theater subscribers, people who bought the tickets long in advance and so felt they had to go, even though they did not want to.

When they had all found their seats and the house lights were dimmed, everyone in the audience was fully expecting to be totally bored (some of them were even hoping to get in a nap and had brought along neck pillows). So they were totally shocked when, as soon as the curtain opened, they were showered with the sparks of a thousand fireworks and deafened by cannon fire while a giant bear shot down from the back of the theater on a flying fox, screaming, "Nay, answer me: stand, and unfold yourself!"

Nanny Piggins's *Hamlet* had begun. It is amazing what stunts, pyrotechnics, and a real motorcycle chase through the audience can do to liven up sixteenth-century literature. Nanny Piggins had written out Hamlet's drippy girlfriend, Ophelia, and replaced her with the much more exciting Phillipa, a motorcycle-riding guitar player who runs off and leaves Hamlet so she can become an astronaut. She got rid of the bit where Hamlet was rude to his mother and put in a scene where Hamlet's mother gave him a stern talking-to about always showing appropriate respect to women. And she replaced the bloodthirsty ending where everyone gets stabbed with a happy ending where everyone gets cake. Altogether it was the most wonderful, touching, rollicking play ever performed anywhere in any language.

After laughing, then crying, then laughing some more, the audience got to their feet and gave a cheering standing ovation. Everyone, including Mrs. Fortescue-Brown, was in one-hundred-percent agreement that it was the best play ever.

So Nanny Piggins, Boris, and the children returned home in high spirits. Even Mr. Green was happy. Everyone had said he was very convincing as a tree.

"That was amazing!" gushed Michael.

"I never knew theater could be so exciting and dangerous!" exclaimed Samantha delightedly while holding an ice pack to her forehead, where she had been struck by a rogue firework.

"It's just a shame you can never perform Nanny Piggins's *Hamlet* again," said Derrick.

For when the owner of the theater had arrived, he was horrified to see the hole in the roof (where Nanny Piggins had been fired out of a cannon for her curtain call), the motorcycle track marks torn into the carpet where

Phillipa had made her dramatic exit to join NASA, and the fire brigade putting out the curtain that had caught alight during the grand cake-eating finale, which naturally involved even more fireworks. The theater owner had made Nanny Piggins promise to never ever direct, produce, or star in any production of any theatrical performance ever again. And since Nanny Piggins believed in making your exit while your audience still held you in awed amazement, she agreed.

"It's for the best," said Nanny Piggins. "If you put on a play that good, everyone will want to see it. It would be cruel to the public to do any less than five performances a night. And a workload that great would become exhausting after five or six years. No, better to retire now, knowing I have written and performed the world's greatest play."

"With a little help from Shakespeare," reminded Samantha.

"Hmm, a *little*," muttered Nanny Piggins.

CHAPTER FIVE

Nanny Piggins and the Runaway Lion

anny Piggins and the children were putting the finishing touches on a beautiful wedding cake. No one they knew was getting married, but Nanny Piggins was not going to let a little thing like that stop them from enjoying a seven-tier chocolate cake with marzipan icing and handmade sugar flowers. The four of them had been making the cake all morning long. It would have been finished sooner, but they kept stopping to eat all the ingredients (they'd had to go back to the supermarket three times already). Plus they each had to take turns hugging Boris and handing him tissues as he sat crying in the corner, because he was Russian and weddings always made him emotional.

So Derrick and Samantha were holding a ladder while Nanny Piggins stood on the top step and reached precariously across to pipe the words *I love cake* on the center of the uppermost layer when, suddenly, Mr. Green burst in through the back door, banging into the stepladder and knocking Nanny Piggins to the floor. (Fortunately she was a flying pig, so she landed gracefully on her bottom.)

"Quick, hide! Nowhere is safe! It's all over the news! We're all doomed!" shrieked Mr. Green as he ran down the corridor, up the stairs, and into his bedroom, where he slammed the door and locked it.

"What on earth has happened to your father?" asked Nanny Piggins as she picked herself up and dusted off her dress. "He's even ruder than normal."

"Perhaps he's finally snapped," suggested Michael.

"Or perhaps he's being audited," guessed Samantha, knowing nothing frightened her father more.

"Or perhaps he needs a hug," said Boris. (Being a bear, bear-hugging was his solution to most problems.)

"Maybe we should watch the news and see what he's all worked up about," suggested Derrick.

So the five of them sat down to watch TV. Nanny Piggins did not normally approve of watching the news because it was always miserable and there were often disturbing images that put you off whatever you were eating. Plus they insisted on giving all the sports scores at the end, which always made Nanny Piggins's eyes roll back into her head from boredom. But on this occasion, the first news item was indeed shocking, and they could soon see why Mr. Green was behaving like an even bigger cowardly custard than normal.

"A large female lion was seen walking through a shopping center earlier this morning," announced the news anchor. "Citizens are urged to remain calm and stay indoors until the animal has been captured."

"Those are our shops!" exclaimed Samantha, as they watched grainy footage of the rear end of a lion disappearing into their local bookstore, which was right next door to the supermarket where they had bought one hundred pounds of sugar, thirty bags of flour, and five blocks of chocolate (to eat on the way home) earlier that morning.

"Should we lock all the doors and windows?" Derrick panicked.

"Pish!" said Nanny Piggins. "It's only a lion. And besides, there's something about that lion...she looks familiar."

"I know what you mean," agreed Boris. "We could only see her hind leg. And it was very fuzzy. But there was something about that fuzzy hind leg..."

Suddenly there was a knock at the door.

"It's the lion!" shrieked Samantha as she flung herself facedown on the sofa and hid her head under a pillow. She was so afraid of being savaged to death by an African wildcat she was not thinking straight, or she would have realized there was no way a pillow could protect her.

"A lion wouldn't knock on the door, silly," said Michael.

"I don't see why not," said Nanny Piggins. "How else do they let people know when they want to be let in?"

"Why don't we look out the window?" suggested Derrick. "That way no one has to open the door and risk getting eaten."

"Good thinking," agreed Nanny Piggins.

So Derrick peeked out through the lace curtains.

"If it is a lion," added Nanny Piggins, "she would be most welcome to have the steak I bought for Mr. Green's dinner."

"It's not. It's a man dressed in some sort of military uniform," said Derrick.

Now it was Nanny Piggins's turn to leap up in panic. "The military! How did they find out I was here?!" she exclaimed.

"What have you done to upset the military?" asked Samantha. She was starting to hyperventilate now. It was hard to worry about so many things at once.

"I can't tell you; it's classified," said Nanny Piggins furtively, as she ran about the room stuffing things into her handbag. "But suffice it to say, I may have accidentally given away military secrets to a foreign government in exchange for a particularly delicious slice of tea cake."

Bang, bang, bang—the man beat on the door. "Sarah Piggins, I know you are in there. You will answer the door!" he ordered in a strange foreign accent.

"Well, good-bye, children, it's been a pleasure being your nanny. I'll miss you terribly, but I will write as soon as I get to South America," said Nanny Piggins as she rushed toward the back door.

"Hang on!" said Boris, grabbing his sister by the collar. "Don't you recognize that voice?"

"What?" said Nanny Piggins, her feet dangling in the air.

"I will count to three, then this door shall be opened," said the man on the doorstep. "One ... two ..."

"Of course! I'd recognize that Danish accent anywhere! It's not the military!" exclaimed Nanny Piggins. "It's the Lion Tamer from the circus!"

Boris put his sister down, and she rushed over to throw open the front door. "Jasper, darling! How are you?" said Nanny Piggins.

The Lion Tamer bowed politely, clicking his heels together, then bent low to kiss the back of Nanny Piggins's trotter.

"Piggins, we meet again," said the Lion Tamer.

"Why is he wearing jodhpurs, knee-high leather boots, and a military jacket?" Samantha whispered to Boris, thinking that the Lion Tamer looked even more frightening than her math teacher.

"He just likes to dress that way," said Boris. "You get all sorts in the circus. Just because the bearded lady looks the strangest, doesn't mean she is the strangest, if you know what I mean."

The children did not know what he meant. But they nodded anyway, hoping they would be able to figure it out for themselves later on.

"So how are things at the circus?" asked Nanny Piggins as she led the Lion Tamer into the living room.

"The Ringmaster, he is an idiot," said the Lion Tamer.

"Of course, that goes without saying," agreed Nanny Piggins.

"And I have some small trouble with one of my girls," said the Lion Tamer.

"Ah yes, we just saw on the news," said Nanny Piggins.

"That was one of the lions from the circus?!" asked Samantha, slightly relieved. If it was a circus lion, perhaps it would not bite her in two; it would just leap through a flaming hoop instead.

"*Ja,*" said the Lion Tamer (because that is how Danish people say *yes*). "It was Ethel. She has run away from home."

"Ethel!" exclaimed Nanny Piggins. "Surely you mean Cassandra or Amy? They're the naughty ones. Ethel was always so easygoing."

"She was the one who got me into yoga," agreed Boris. "She's really in touch with both her yin and her yang."

"It *is* Ethel," snapped the Lion Tamer. "I know this for a fact because she left a very rude letter."

"What did it say?" asked Nanny Piggins. She always enjoyed rude letters. She particularly liked writing them herself. But reading ones written to other people was fun too.

"I burned it," said the Lion Tamer.

"Did you memorize it first?" asked Nanny Piggins hopefully.

"The letter is gone. And so is Ethel," said the Lion Tamer. He then began to do the most startling thing. He started to shudder violently and make a barking noise like a seal. It was several moments before the others realized what he was doing. The Lion Tamer was crying. (It is a sad fact that a lot of men are very bad at crying. Which is why they really should practice more. That way they will not look silly when they try it.)

"She says she is running away to a petting zoo in Tanzania," sobbed the Lion Tamer.

"Who would put a lion in a petting zoo?" Michael whispered to Boris.

"Someone who doesn't like children," suggested Boris.

"There, there." Nanny Piggins comforted the Lion Tamer. "I'm sure she won't really. After all, Ethel doesn't speak Swahili. And I know for a fact she can't stand missing an episode of *The Young and the Irritable*. So there's no way she'd go to Central East Africa without asking you to record it for her."

"I hope you're right," sniffed the Lion Tamer. "I miss my little kitty cat." He burst into tears again.

"Why don't you re-catch Ethel and tell her how you feel?" asked Nanny Piggins.

"It is embarrassing," said the Lion Tamer, blowing his nose and trying to regather some of his dignity. "I cannot let her see me like this. A Lion Tamer must maintain strict discipline at all times."

"Come now, that's no excuse," said Nanny Piggins.

"Also, I tried already," admitted the Lion Tamer, "but Ethel will not come when I call."

Nanny Piggins and Boris gasped.

"But she's a lion and you are the Lion Tamer. It's her job to obey you," said Boris.

"I know. That is what I said, but she won't listen to

me," said the Lion Tamer. "That is why I came to you. When you were at the circus, Ethel was a particular friend of yours. So please, I'm begging you to help me. Help me bring my Ethel home."

"Of course," said Nanny Piggins. "You lie down quietly and have a pack of chocolate cookies. Come along, children, fetch your father's car keys. We've got a lion to catch."

"Shouldn't we get some sort of protective gear first? Perhaps a motorcycle helmet or a Kevlar vest?" asked Samantha.

"Oh, no, there's no point bothering with that," laughed Boris. "A lion would just rip it right off. No, the only hope you have with a lion is to be polite."

"And hope they've just eaten a large meal," added Nanny Piggins.

And so Nanny Piggins, Boris, and the children climbed into Mr. Green's vomit-yellow Rolls-Royce and set out in search of Ethel the lion.

"Where do we look first?" asked Derrick.

"Well, we know not to look for her in the bookstore,"

said Nanny Piggins, "because she was there this morning."

"But what if she didn't like the book she bought and wanted to return it?" suggested Boris.

"Good point," conceded Nanny Piggins.

So they drove to the bookstore. When they got there, they found the owner drinking a cup of tea, but his hand was shaking so badly, he was getting more on the counter than in his mouth. In between the stuttering and the weeping, he was able to tell them that a terrifyingly ferocious lion matching Ethel's description had bought an English-to-Swahili dictionary earlier that morning. (And she must have been happy with it because she had not brought it back.)

"But Ethel isn't terrifying or ferocious," protested Boris.

"There must be another lion on the loose!" exclaimed Nanny Piggins.

"Or perhaps it was Ethel, and she seemed terrifying to him," suggested Michael as he patted the shopkeeper's shoulder supportively.

"It is normal for people to be frightened of lions," added Derrick as he used a copy of *Great Expectations* to mop up the spilt tea.

"And she might be in a ferocious mood if she was angry enough to run away from the circus," worried Samantha.

"I suppose," conceded Nanny Piggins, "but I don't know why you'd be afraid of lions when there are much more frightening beasts wandering loose—like dieticians!"

Boris shuddered. "Imagine bumping into a dietician when you weren't expecting it."

"Shhh," cautioned Nanny Piggins. "We'd better stop talking about it or we'll give the children nightmares."

Nanny Piggins, Boris, and the children got back in the Rolls-Royce and continued searching. "Where to next?" asked Michael.

"The butcher shop, I think," said Nanny Piggins.

"In case Ethel's hungry?" asked Samantha.

"No, in case she's looking for a job," explained Nanny Piggins. "Who's better at tearing up raw meat than a lion?"

When they got to the butcher shop, they found the butcher curled up in the corner, rocking back and forth.

"He looks very frightened," said Derrick.

"Perhaps he's just read an article about the rise of veg-etarianism," suggested Nanny Piggins.

"Or perhaps he's just seen Ethel," suggested Michael more realistically.

"He's right!" called Boris. "Ethel has been here! Look, she left her résumé on the counter."

Nanny Piggins read it. "Let's see: a gap year working as an au pair in France, two years working as a stockbroker on Wall Street, and eight and a half years being tamed at the circus. That's Ethel all right!"

"Sh-sh-she just c-came in here," stuttered the butcher. (He had been coaxed out of his catatonic state by Samantha offering him a bite of her chocolate bar.) "She a-a-asked about a job, l-l-left a résumé, and then bought half a side of b-b-beef, because she said she was p-p-peckish."

"How did she pay for it?" asked Michael.

"C-c-cash," jittered the butcher.

"But how can a lion have money?" asked Derrick.

"She gets a wage at the circus," said Nanny Piggins.

"I thought the Ringmaster didn't like paying people," said Samantha.

"He always pays the lions. He might be an idiot, but he's not entirely stupid," explained Nanny Piggins. "Plus Ethel has always been very good at following the stock market. She has quite the investment portfolio."

"How can a lion have an investment portfolio? Apart from being a lion, she lives in a traveling circus," said Samantha.

"Just because you're on the road doesn't mean you can't read the financial papers," said Nanny Piggins.

"But *you're* not rich," said Derrick.

"True," agreed Nanny Piggins. "My chocolate habit is a tremendous financial burden. But in life, some things are worth the sacrifice."

The children nodded. This was a statement whose wisdom they could fully understand.

"So where should we look for Ethel next?" asked Boris.

"I'm not sure," said Nanny Piggins. "Perhaps we should just walk around a bit. Maybe we'll bump into her."

The thought of "bumping into" a lion only made Samantha want to barricade herself in the butcher's cold-storage room. But after the others pried her fingers off the counter one at a time and promised Samantha that she could climb up on Boris's head at the first glimpse of a giant cat, the five of them were eventually able to set out into the shopping precinct on their lion hunt.

They met with almost immediate success when they heard screaming up ahead.

"What could that be?" asked Boris.

"Perhaps a crowd of people are horrified by the produce prices," guessed Nanny Piggins. This was an issue she felt strongly about. She was always astounded the produce department had the audacity to charge anything for brussels sprouts.

"Or perhaps they're frightened because they saw a lion?" suggested Derrick.

"Ah yes, of course. I keep forgetting the silly, irrational reactions you humans have to large meat-eating creatures," said Nanny Piggins.

"I wish I could," said Boris, dabbing a tear from the corner of his eye. It still hurt his feelings every time an old lady screamed and ran away when he offered to help her across the road. Perhaps in the future, he would try walking with them across the road, instead of throwing them. It was being picked up and swung about his head that seemed to alarm them.

Nanny Piggins gave her brother's hand a quick, comforting squeeze, and then they set off following the sound of screaming, which soon led them to the local cinema. Nanny Piggins looked up at the marquee to see what was playing.

"Ahh, *Out of Africa*. No wonder she came here," said Nanny Piggins. "Her uncle has a cameo in this film. Sadly, he never got much more movie work because he was forever typecast as a lion. Anyway, let's go in."

Nanny Piggins, Boris, and the children wandered through the now-deserted lobby. They would have paid for tickets, but they could not, because the ticket collector was hiding under the popcorn stand, refusing to come out.

It was hard to see anything in the darkened cinema. Samantha clutched Boris's hand tightly, wishing she was ten feet tall and over one thousand pounds too so she would not have to be so scared. At first it looked like there was no one in the audience at all. But then they heard the distinctive sound of popcorn being munched. They turned and peered into the darkness. At the very back of the theater, they could just make out the shadowy shape of a lion.

"Hello?" called Nanny Piggins.

"Shhhh," growled Ethel. "I'm trying to watch the movie."

"Ethel, it's Sarah Piggins," called Nanny Piggins.

"Sarah?!" exclaimed Ethel. "And Boris too! How wonderful to see you. You're just in time; the film has only just started."

"We can't watch a movie now," said Nanny Piggins. "The Lion Tamer is at our house, and he wants you to come back to the circus."

"Hah!" said Ethel (all circus performers have an excellent sense of the dramatic). "I'll bet he does. Well, I'm not coming back. He's a big meanie, and I've had enough of it. So there." With that, Ethel stuffed another handful of popcorn in her mouth and glared at the movie screen, ignoring Nanny Piggins.

"Children, I think you and Boris had better wait out-side," said Nanny Piggins.

Samantha could not have been more grateful for this suggestion. She practically ran out the exit, screaming.

"It's time Ethel and me had a serious lion-to-pig con-versation," said Nanny Piggins.

So Boris and the children waited outside, where they had a lovely time playing hopscotch on the sticky carpet (which all cinemas seem to have) and eating candy from the snack bar (for which the staff were too frightened to make them pay). When Nanny Piggins and Ethel finally emerged, Ethel still looked a little sulky, but Nanny Piggins held her firmly by the hand.

"Come along, children. We're going home," said Nanny Piggins.

"Is Ethel going back to the circus?" asked Derrick.

"We'll see," said Nanny Piggins cryptically.

Amazingly enough, somewhere on the return journey, Samantha completely overcame her fear of being eaten by a lion. Just as people with a fear of flying can conquer their phobia by learning to be a pilot, it turns out you can overcome a fear of lions simply by being squished in the backseat of a Rolls-Royce between a huge bear and a fully grown lioness.

The Lion Tamer was overwhelmed as soon as he saw Ethel. He did not bark like a seal, but his neck did go pink and his chin quivered, which, for him, was a sign of great emotion.

"Oh, Ethel, you naughty girl. I am pleased you have agreed to return," said the Lion Tamer.

The Lion Tamer was overwhelmed
as soon as he saw Ethel.

"Ethel is returning," said Nanny Piggins, "but only if you agree to certain conditions."

"Conditions? What are these *conditions* of which you speak?" asked the Lion Tamer.

"If he has to ask, I'm not telling him," said Ethel sulkily.

"It seems Ethel is not the only one who has been naughty," said Nanny Piggins, fixing the Lion Tamer with her most piercing glare.

"What do you mean?" blustered the Lion Tamer. He might be a brave lion tamer, but like most people, he was still afraid of Nanny Piggins.

"Ethel tells me that you have been ordering her about—telling her to jump through flaming hoops and open her mouth so you can put your head in it," said Nanny Piggins.

"I'm a lion tamer. That is what I do," protested the Lion Tamer.

"But without ever saying 'please'?" asked Nanny Piggins.

The children gasped. They knew it was a terrible sin to ask for something and not say *please*. Nanny Piggins always made a point of saying *please* to the man in the corner shop before she ripped all the chocolate off his shelves, tore open their wrappings, and stuffed the whole lot in her mouth.

"I may have forgotten to say this word once or twice," admitted the Lion Tamer.

"Hah—once or twice?! Try *never*!" accused Ethel.

"And what's this I hear about a whip?" asked Nanny Piggins.

"He's been beating Ethel with a whip?" asked Samantha, astounded that Ethel had merely run away and not eaten the Lion Tamer first.

"No, worse. He's been cracking it near me. He knows I don't like loud noises. It's terrible for my nerves," complained Ethel.

"You brute," reproached Nanny Piggins.

"But this is what all the lion tamers do," protested the Lion Tamer.

"That is no excuse. If all the lion tamers jumped in a lake, would you do that too?" asked Nanny Piggins.

"No," pouted the Lion Tamer. Now it was his turn to sulk.

"I should think not," said Nanny Piggins.

"So aren't you coming back to the circus, then?" the

Lion Tamer asked Ethel. "What am I going to do without you? You're my best lion. Cassy and Amy can't do a triple somersault backward through a burning hoop, no matter how much I waggle a chair in their faces."

"Ethel has agreed to return under certain conditions," said Nanny Piggins, taking a piece of paper out of her pocket, unfolding it, and reading aloud. "Number one, she gets to hold the whip and the chair every second night."

"What?" exclaimed the Lion Tamer.

"It's only fair you take turns," said Nanny Piggins sternly.

"I suppose," said the Lion Tamer. "All right, I agree."

"Number two," continued Nanny Piggins. "You have to give her a big hug and say 'Well done' at the end of every performance."

"But what will the other lion tamers say?!" complained the Lion Tamer.

"If your friends expect you to be rude, then perhaps you need to make new friends," said Nanny Piggins.

The Lion Tamer hung his head. He knew she was right. Lion tamers could be a very bad influence. "All right," he conceded.

"And finally, she wants a bright red convertible sports car," said Nanny Piggins.

"What?!" exploded the Lion Tamer. "I can't afford that!"

"That's all right," said Nanny Piggins. "Ethel is very good with money. She will work out a payment plan for you so you can manage it on your income."

"Det er latterligt!" exclaimed the Lion Tamer (which is Danish for "this is ridiculous").

"Do you want Ethel back or not?" asked Nanny Piggins.

"All right, I agree to it all," said the Lion Tamer, knowing when he was beaten. He turned to Ethel. "It is so good to have you back." Then the Lion Tamer gave Ethel a big hug, even though she had not done a show yet.

To celebrate, they all ate the seven-tier wedding cake (which just goes to show, if you bake a cake you will always find a reason for eating it) before Ethel and the Lion Tamer went home to the circus.

Their new arrangement was immediately a huge success. The crowds thought a lioness brandishing a whip and chair at a Lion Tamer and making him jump through hoops was a wonderfully ironic, postmodern statement. So all the shows in which Ethel tamed the Lion Tamer quickly sold out. Pretty soon the Lion Tamer had to give up his turn holding the whip and chair completely. Ethel wrote and told Nanny Piggins all about it in a letter.

"Do you think Ethel is happy?" asked Samantha.

"Oh yes, I should think she's having a marvelous time," said Nanny Piggins. "Although we should keep the guest room ready."

"Why?" asked Michael.

"From the sound of it, the Lion Tamer might be running away soon," explained Nanny Piggins.

So they kept a pack of chocolate cookies and a full box of tissues in the guest room, just in case.

CHAPTER SIX

Nanny Piggins Joins the Ski Team

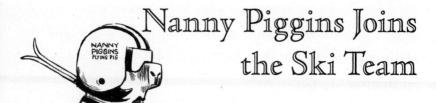

Y ou children are very lucky," began Mr. Green pompously. Derrick, Samantha, Michael, and Nanny Piggins immediately froze mid-breakfast.

"What have you done this time?" glowered Nanny Piggins.

"You can't send us to work in a sweatshop," said Derrick. "You know what the social worker said last time you tried."

"Yes, well…" muttered Mr. Green. He did not like to

think about that incident. The social worker had yelled at him for several hours using the words "ashamed" and "disgraceful" repeatedly. "No, this is all aboveboard. I have arranged for a sports scout to come and inspect you."

"You've done what?" asked Nanny Piggins. She was perplexed. Mr. Green had never shown any interest in sports before.

"I met a talent scout from the National Sports School. He says that if you get any child young enough, you can train them up to international standards. And you three are young, so I told him you would be most suitable," explained Mr. Green as he shoved another whole-wheat muffin into his mouth.

"Which sport are we trying out for?" asked Derrick.

"I don't know," said Mr. Green dismissively. "He'll measure you and make you run about a bit, I expect. Then he'll come to some decision."

"I suppose that wouldn't be too bad," said Nanny Piggins to the children reassuringly, "so long as he picks you for a nice sport like rowing, where you get to sit down and keep snacks in the boat."

But Samantha suspected Mr. Green's true motivation.

"Father, where is the National Sports School exactly?" she asked.

Mr. Green smiled, totally failing to hide his glee. "Four hundred and twenty-three miles away. I measured it on a map," he said triumphantly.

"But it will take forever for them to get there and back every day on the bus," protested Nanny Piggins.

"It's a boarding school," said Mr. Green. "If they get in, they have to live there. They even get to stay during school vacations to do extra jogging."

"What?" exploded Nanny Piggins.

The doorbell rang, saving Mr. Green from the full brunt of Nanny Piggins's temper.

"That will be him now," said Mr. Green, getting to his feet.

"How long have you been planning this?" Nanny Piggins called after him.

"Oh, just a few months," admitted Mr. Green as he slipped out of the room to let the scout in.

"What are we going to do?" asked Derrick.

"What if they make us do sit-ups?!" exclaimed Samantha.

"Should we make a run for it?" suggested Michael.

"No, the scout might see you and put you on the marathon team," said Nanny Piggins. "You'd better just play along with it for now. I'll think of something. Don't worry, I won't let them take you to a sports school. I barely think it's suitable for you to go to a regular school."

And so the children went out into the back garden with their father and the sports scout. It was not too awful at first. The scout just measured them, saying things like, "Hmm, good pole-vaulting legs there," and "Yes, nice stumpy netball fingers," and "Excellent discus thrower's ankles." But then he started making them do horrible things like run in circles and do as many push-ups as they could until their arms collapsed.

Nanny Piggins and Boris watched from the rooftop. Mr. Green had banned Nanny Piggins from going into the back garden. He correctly anticipated that she would try to sabotage the process. Indeed, she was just wondering whether she would get in trouble if she threw her binoculars at Mr. Green's head, when the most spectacular thing happened.

Now, Mr. Green was not a man who believed in paying for home maintenance, so the roof had not been retiled for many years. That said, even a brand-new roof is not designed to hold a thousand-pound-plus dancing bear who was, at that very moment, choreographing a dramatic ballet to express the unhappy emotions he felt as he watched the poor Green children being forced to do exercise. And so just as Boris did a grand jeté (which is ballet talk for "flying leap"), the roof collapsed under him, sending Boris hurtling down through the attic, smashing through the ceiling, and landing safely on the soft mattress in Nanny Piggins's bedroom.

But Nanny Piggins was not so lucky. The tiles her brother had dislodged were sent flying in every direction so that the roof quite literally slipped out from under her, shooting her down the steep gable and out into the air, two stories above the ground.

The children gasped in horror as they saw their nanny come hurtling toward the earth. Mr. Green gasped in horror as his brain calculated how much it would cost to replace the roof tiles. And the sports scout stared in openmouthed awe, having never seen such an impeccably dressed pig come shooting off a roof before.

But then an even more amazing thing happened. Nanny Piggins tucked in her trotters, curled up into a ball, spun around three times, stretched out into a perfect swan dive, and landed effortlessly on the lawn as though this was the type of thing she did every day.

"Wow!" said Derrick.

Samantha was too shocked and Michael too impressed to speak.

"You could have crushed my gladioli," grumbled Mr. Green.

But then the scout stumbled forward, knocking Mr. Green out of the way, and clutched Nanny Piggins by the shoulders. "That was the single most impressive feat of athleticism I have seen in all my forty years as a sports scout," he said.

"I'm not surprised," said Nanny Piggins. For she was an honest pig, and she knew her flying abilities were second to none.

"I'm begging you, you have to join the national ski

jumping team today," said the scout. (He actually got down on his knees and clutched her trotters as he said this.)

"But what about the children?" spluttered Mr. Green angrily. "It's them you're meant to be taking away."

"They're nice kids," said the scout, "but they've got about as much sporting talent as an avocado. I couldn't do anything with them."

"What a relief," said Samantha. She had been terrified they were going to force her to play hockey. She had a dread fear of being hit in the shins with a stick.

"But if you take the nanny, who will look after the children?" protested Mr. Green, looking like he was about to cry.

"It's all right; I'll take them with me," said Nanny Piggins. "I wouldn't leave them here with you."

"Oh, that's all right, then," said Mr. Green, suddenly happy again. "Well, I'll leave you all to it. I knew this was a good idea of mine." And with that, he ran to his car, which actually caused the scout to raise an eyebrow, because Mr. Green could put on some serious speed when he was trying to get away from his children.

"You must fly out to the Italian Alps immediately to

meet the rest of the team and commence training," said the scout.

"What exactly will Nanny Piggins be training for?" asked Derrick.

"The World Championships are in two weeks. And our best ski jumper broke his leg yesterday when he tried to kick a cat and fell down a flight of stairs," explained the scout.

"It just goes to show, cruelty to animals never pays," said Nanny Piggins wisely. "Except for my sister Wendy, who is a nasty piece of work and deserves a good pinch should you ever meet her."

"We never thought we'd find a replacement in time, but as soon as I saw you fall off that roof…" said the scout, struggling to find the words to express his awe. "It's almost as if you could fly."

"Oh, I can," said Nanny Piggins truthfully.

So the next day Nanny Piggins, Boris, and the children arrived in the Italian Alps. Boris had had to travel in the hold, which made Nanny Piggins angry. Just because her brother was ten feet tall and weighed over a thousand pounds did not mean he was not entitled to bad airline food like the rest of the passengers. But Boris did not mind. He enjoyed flying in the hold. He liked going through all the other passengers' suitcases and trying on their clothes. Sadly, nothing ever fit. But Boris was an optimistic bear and would not rest until he had stretched or torn every item of clothing trying.

When Nanny Piggins and her entourage arrived at the hotel, the rest of the ski jumping team was not immediately impressed.

"But you're a girl!" protested the coach.

"And a pig!" complained the team captain.

"I know," said Nanny Piggins. "It hardly seems fair. I have twice as many legs as you so that doubles the number of ways I can make a landing. But we read the rules carefully and they didn't say anything specifically excluding pigs."

"Only sheep," supplied Derrick.

"Which is understandable," said Boris. "Sheep are very nice, but silly creatures. And they cheat."

"And so, here I am," said Nanny Piggins.

"What's the farthest you've ever jumped?" asked the captain, glaring at his new teammate.

"She made forty-five feet when she fell off the roof," said Michael proudly.

"Don't tell me you've never been off a proper ski jump?!" exclaimed the coach.

"I've never even skied," admitted Nanny Piggins.

"This is ridiculous!" said the captain.

The other ski jumpers from the team muttered grumpily.

"Why don't you give Nanny Piggins a chance?" urged Samantha. "She'll surprise you."

"Good idea," decided the coach. "If she breaks her neck we definitely won't have to have her on the team."

So Nanny Piggins, Boris, the children, and the entire national ski jumping team trudged up the snowy staircase to the top of the ski jump. There were a lot of stairs. This irritated Nanny Piggins. If she had known they would have to walk so far in an upward direction, she would have packed more snacks. As it was she made everyone stop for a cake break twice along the way (fortunately she had two large mud cakes in her handbag).

When they got to the top and looked down, the children were terrified. The ski jump was so long and steep, they did not see how jumping off it could possibly be a sport. It looked about as safe as leaping off a fifteen-story building. But Nanny Piggins was unperturbed.

"Is that all?" she asked dismissively. "Haven't you got a higher one?"

The captain ignored her bravado. "Do you want me to run you through the basics?" he asked. Because he was not really a bad person, and he did not want to get in trouble for accidental pig-icide.

"Young man," said Nanny Piggins scornfully as she drew herself up to her full four feet of height. "There is nothing *you* could teach *me* about flying." Then she thought better of it. "Actually, yes, there is. Could you show me how to put the skis on?"

So after the coach and the captain strapped the skis to Nanny Piggins's feet, which took a lot of duct tape because ski boots are not designed to fit trotters (an oversight the manufacturers really should remedy),

Nanny Piggins stood atop the ski jump. She looked spectacular. She was wearing her flying pig costume from the circus. It was made of skintight yellow leather with black and red stripes down both sides and held a helmet that had NANNY PIGGINS—FLYING PIG written on it in rhinestones.

Even the callous coach started to feel bad as he watched the petite and glamorous pig standing on the precipice, the wind rippling through her perfectly coiffured hair.

"You don't have to do this, you know," said the captain. "You can just ask the Ski Jumping Association to send you home. I'm sure they won't fine you or anything."

Nanny Piggins turned and looked the captain in the eye. "If I don't jump, will I have to walk all the way back down those stairs?" she asked.

"Yes," replied the captain.

"Piffle to that!" said Nanny Piggins. With which she turned to face the valley, put on her helmet, and pushed off the edge.

The children held their breath. Not out of fear, but from sheer admiration. Because as soon as Nanny

139

Piggins set off, it was clear she knew exactly what she was doing. Their nanny gave herself over to gravity and hurtled down the slope, her body extended forward, leaning into the wind. By the time she shot off the end of the jump, she had transformed herself into the shape of a bullet. Her snout stretched forward so she cut through the air like a hot knife through butter. The ski jumpers and coaching staff stared in astounded awe.

"She's never going to land," exclaimed the captain.

"That is the most beautiful ski jump I have ever seen!" exclaimed the coach.

But their admiration was soon interrupted by a more serious realization.

"She's going to hit the ski lodge!" screamed Samantha.

And Samantha was right. Nanny Piggins's ski jump was so good that she was not going to land in the landing area. She was going to overshoot it entirely and hit the ski lodge behind.

"What are we going to do?" asked Derrick, totally at a loss because his nanny was not there to tell him.

"I can't look," said Samantha, although she was so paralyzed with fear she could not move the muscles to close her eyes.

"That is the most beautiful ski jump I have ever seen!" exclaimed the coach.

"It's all right," yelled Michael. "I think she's aiming for it!"

And indeed Nanny Piggins was. If the ski jumpers had not seen it for themselves, they would never have believed it. For Nanny Piggins gracefully touched down just in front of the ski lodge, where she slid across the veranda and into the downstairs bar. Everyone was silent for a moment as they waited to hear the inevitable crash. But there was none.

"Quick, we've got to see if she's all right," said Derrick.

The children and the ski jumping team hastily ran down the stairs and through the snow to the lodge to check on Nanny Piggins. But they need not have worried. By the time they got inside, they found Nanny Piggins dancing along the bar, drinking hot chocolate and singing alpine folk songs, much to the delight of the other patrons.

"You're alive!" said Samantha.

"Of course I'm alive," said Nanny Piggins, "although I was worried there for a moment. I thought I was going to miss the ski lodge, which would have been terrible because I was starving."

And so, having witnessed her superior ability, the other ski jumpers immediately embraced Nanny Piggins as a fellow team member. They wanted to make her team captain but she refused, because captains had to give interviews to journalists, and she always found it hard not to bite journalists on the legs (they are such terrible liars). She did, however, find time to totally overhaul the sport of ski jumping.

For starters, she convinced the ski jumpers to follow her own training regimen, which was to sleep as late as possible, to eat everything you can, and to do absolutely no weight training, fitness training, or ski training at all.

"It is very, very important to be well rested," advised Nanny Piggins. "If you are going to win, you will need all your energy. And if you are going to lose, you might as well look fabulous, which means no bags under your eyes."

She also completely changed the team's diet. The first thing she did was fire the team's macrobiotic chef. It took some time to explain to Nanny Piggins what a macrobiotic chef was, but as soon as she understood that he believed in eating organic vegetables and avoiding refined sugar, she chased him around the kitchen seven times, taking swipes at him with his own soup ladle. Nanny Piggins did not usually believe in violence, but cruelty to food brought out her disciplinarian side. She instituted a strict high-calorie diet for all the athletes and coaching staff (which made her instantly beloved). She insisted on them eating double the amount of chocolate and cake she would normally recommend because they had been on macrobiotics for so long she needed to undo the damage.

And so, when the team arrived at the World Championships two weeks later, they were happier and fatter than they had ever been before. And in a sport that involves plummeting, a few extra pounds do not hurt.

The Russians and the Norwegians were their main competitors, and when they saw Nanny Piggins arrive at the ski jumping venue, they laughed openly. If Nanny Piggins had not had such a lovely time drinking hot chocolate and singing alpine folk songs for the past two weeks, she might have thought about punishing them. As it was, she knew that being beaten by a flying pig would be punishment enough.

The morning of the big competition soon arrived.

"Are you nervous?" asked Derrick.

"Why would I feel nervous?" replied Nanny Piggins. "Obviously I feel bad for the other competitors because they will shortly be made to look like fools on international television. But I don't think they'll attack me. They'll probably just cry a lot and never want to see snow again."

Now, the way the Ski Jump World Championships works is that each athlete gets two jumps. The distances are measured and points are given for form and style by an international panel of judges. Then all those numbers are combined in a complicated way that nobody quite understands by someone in a back room with a calculator, and that is how the winner is decided.

The competition started early in the morning, but it took quite a while to get through all the athletes because the ones who jumped well took forever celebrating by pumping their fists in the air and showing off in front of the crowd, and the ones who jumped badly had to be scraped off the bottom of the hillside by an ambulance crew. Nanny Piggins was scheduled to jump last because no one had ever heard of her before, and if she made a botch of it they did not want her to damage the ramp before everybody else had had their turn.

So by the time Nanny Piggins stepped out onto the top of the ski jump, the Norwegians were in the lead, with the Russians close behind. She was again wearing her bright yellow jumping suit (Nanny Piggins was excused from wearing the team colors because she undeniably looked fabulous in yellow).

In the dressing shed behind her, Nanny Piggins could hear the Norwegian coach snickering with the Russian coach. One of them even had the audacity to make an oinking noise. Nanny Piggins made a mental note to deal with them later. But she was not going to be distracted now, because the crisp alpine air smelled clean and pure, and the updraft was strong and welcoming. The mountain was practically calling to her, saying, "Jump, Nanny Piggins, jump."

And so she did. Nanny Piggins pushed herself off the edge, crouched low while she built up momentum, and then launched off the end of the jump like a rocket.

There were no cheers, no boos, and definitely no oinking noises. The crowd of ten thousand people watched Nanny Piggins fly through the air in completely silent awe. That was until the people in the main stand at the bottom realized she was going to overshoot the landing area (again) and crash into them. At this point people started screaming and trying to get out of the way.

But they should have had more faith in the world's greatest flying pig. The people in the top row at the back just heard her say, "Duck, please!" as she shot through where they had been sitting, missing the back of their seats by less than a whisker.

She then flew another fifty yards before landing in the drive-through lane of a fast-food restaurant, a block down the street. Naturally she picked up two dozen Merry Meals for herself, the children, Boris, and the rest of the team before walking back.

The crowd roared cheers of approval as she reentered the stadium. Even the people who had been forced to evacuate their seats did not mind. They had a story they would be able to tell their grandchildren in years to come—the time they had nearly been hit in the head by the world's greatest ski jumping pig.

The Russians and the Norwegians did not look so smug now. They were too busy reading the rulebook, triple-checking to see if you really could enter a female pig in the Ski Jump World Championships.

"You did it, Nanny Piggins," yelled Derrick excitedly. "You jumped farther than anyone else ever has in the history of the ski jump."

"Really?" said Nanny Piggins. "I wondered why they built that stand so close. It makes you wonder why all these silly men go into ski jumping if they're so bad at it. Perhaps it's just because they like the skintight bodysuits?"

"Your first jump was so much farther than anybody else, you only have to complete your second jump, and you'll win," said Michael excitedly. He'd brought along a calculator and worked that out himself.

The second round was held that afternoon. Nanny Piggins spent the interim signing autographs and eating chocolate to gird her energy.

All the other competitors did their jumps and tried their best, but their hearts were not in it. As Nanny Piggins had predicted, many of them were already crying and planning to give the sport up, having seen their entire life's work trounced by a female pig.

The Norwegian and Russian coaches scowled at Nanny Piggins as she walked toward the top of the jump carrying her skis. This time she did stop to speak to them.

"Gentlemen, I know competitive sports bring out the worst in humans, but in the future I advise you not to engage in pig-ist behavior. It is unseemly. And as a pig, it is wearisome having to constantly be putting silly men in their place."

"We don't know what you're talking about," protested the Russian coach.

"Then let me explain," said Nanny Piggins menacingly. "If I hear an *oink* out of either of you again, you'll soon be making a very different noise when I sink my teeth into your shins."

With that, Nanny Piggins strode out onto the ski jump.

"You can do it, Nanny Piggins," encouraged Derrick.

"We're so proud of you," called Samantha.

"Throw in a somersault," requested Michael.

"And see if you can land in the ice-cream shop this time," called Boris. "I fancy a scoop of tutti-frutti!"

Nanny Piggins gave her entourage a thumbs-up, then

turned to look down the slope. She saw the crowd (now fifteen thousand strong, because people had jumped in their cars and driven over to see the flying pig), and she found the spot she was aiming for—the back row of the stands, now vacated in anticipation. Then she launched herself into the jump.

Nanny Piggins whistled down the ramp even faster than before, her ears drawn tight against her head and her snout stretched forward for maximum aerodynamics. Then, at just the right moment, she used her hind legs to thrust herself forward off the jump. And she was flying.

The people from the back row of the stands knew they could have kept their seats, because Nanny Piggins was going even farther this time. The penthouse suite of the tallest hotel in town was about to get a flying pig come crashing in through its window. That was, until it happened...

Someone opened a chocolate bar.

Now the sound of a chocolate bar wrapper being torn open is very distinctive. And Nanny Piggins's hearing was so good, she could tell the difference between a

Kit Kat and a Mars bar being opened from five miles away. So when she heard that magical noise, she never really made a conscious decision. Her entire body simply responded reflexively, swooping in the general direction of the sound and snapping the chocolate bar out of the hand of its owner, who just happened to be the Norwegian judge who knew full well that leaving the course mid-jump was grounds for immediate disqualification, even if the jumper had been entrapped by a chocolate bar.

The entire crowd groaned with disappointment.

When the children found Nanny Piggins she was sitting in the snow behind the judges' table, trying to lick every last trace of chocolate off the wrapper.

"Oh, Nanny Piggins," sympathized Samantha. "Are you all right?"

Boris did not say anything. He just wrapped his sister in a bear hug.

"Are you dreadfully disappointed to be disqualified and lose out on the gold medal?" asked Derrick.

Nanny Piggins looked up. "Gold medal?" It took her a moment to realize what they were saying. "Why would I worry about that? I've just had the most delicious chocolate bar."

"But, Nanny Piggins," said Michael, "I think that Norwegian judge may have opened the chocolate bar on purpose to trick you into not winning."

"Then he is a very silly man indeed," said Nanny Piggins, "because who got to eat the chocolate bar? Not him! Really, I don't know how these men get to be national officials. Their priorities are all wrong."

"You've been thrown off the national team," said Samantha.

"We have to go back to living with Father," said Derrick.

"It's probably for the best," said Nanny Piggins. "We shouldn't really leave your father unattended for too long. It isn't fair to the rest of the community. And ski jumping is exhausting."

"But you never do any training or practice," said Michael.

"I know, but being universally admired is hard work,"

explained Nanny Piggins. "Besides, I much prefer being a nanny. It's more exciting."

And so Nanny Piggins, Boris, and the children headed home that afternoon, satisfied that they had enjoyed a lovely two-week vacation and completely revolution-ized the sport of ski jumping at the same time.

CHAPTER SEVEN

Nanny Piggins:
A Biography

ow dare you suggest such a price!" yelled Nanny Piggins.

"You are trying to ruin me!" accused the shopkeeper.

Boris and the children were standing on the sixth floor of a restaurant supply shop in Chinatown watching Nanny Piggins haggle over the price of a new wok.[2] It was quite a show.

---

[2] A wok is a large, round-bottomed Chinese frying pan. If you find that hard to visualize, just imagine a frying pan, and you will be close enough.

"Do you want my family to starve?" demanded the shopkeeper.

"It is the children I care for who will starve if I agree to your extortionate demands," countered Nanny Piggins.

"If you can't afford a wok, maybe you should just eat your food raw!" yelled the shopkeeper.

Nanny Piggins's old wok had been ruined earlier that morning in a backyard badminton accident. She had been using it as a racket (because the badminton rackets were ruined when they played Scott of the Antarctic.[3] They had made excellent snowshoes, but sadly, like Scott, the rackets did not survive).

To win the badminton game, Nanny Piggins had thrown herself full-stretch at the shuttlecock and hit a brilliant volley. Unfortunately Boris was so delighted by his sister's success, he jumped up and down excitedly, accidentally jumping on Nanny Piggins's wok.

---

[3]Robert Falcon Scott was a British Naval Officer who, in 1912, set out to discover the South Pole. After an exhausting, dangerous, and bitterly cold journey, Scott and his team arrived at the South Pole only to discover they had been beaten there by Roald Amundsen by just thirty-three days. Scott and his entire team then died on the return journey. This tragic historical event captured the imagination of the public across the British Empire.

And while woks are designed to withstand incredibly high temperatures and extremely bad-tempered chefs, they are not designed to withstand the full weight of a thousand-pound-plus bear. Which is how she came to be haggling with the shopkeeper.

Now, Nanny Piggins and the shopkeeper both knew what price she would end up paying for the wok, but they both enjoyed haggling. You see, in ordinary day-to-day life it is frowned upon to yell loudly at someone, call them names, and wave your arms about. But when you are haggling, that is all okay.

"You want me to lose my shop and live in a cardboard box on the street," remonstrated the shopkeeper.

"I want you to charge reasonable prices and stop taking advantage of poor hardworking nannies," retorted Nanny Piggins.

But just then their argument was interrupted by the most extraordinary event. Out of the corner of her eye, Nanny Piggins noticed a toddler on a balcony in the building opposite. The toddler, with the total lack of self-preservation unique to children of that age, was climbing over the safety barrier. Nanny Piggins froze mid-haggle and pointed. She was just about to call out,

"Climb back inside, you naughty child," when the little boy lost his grip and fell.

Nanny Piggins did not even think. Her circus training kicked in, and she reacted instinctively by hurling herself out of the window and catching the falling infant. At this point she did allow herself a brief millisecond of self-congratulation before turning her mind to the more urgent matter of what to do about the hard pavement that they were plummeting toward.

Fortunately there were several canvas awnings below her, so, holding the baby tightly in her arms, Nanny Piggins spun around to land flat on her back on the first one. She tore straight through, but the awning had slowed her fall. So when she hit the second awning Nanny Piggins bounced off, spiraling across the street and hitting another awning, which she bounced off too. Now Nanny Piggins was starting to enjoy herself, so she did a double flip before smashing through a fourth awning feetfirst, and landing on a street cart full of bananas.

Nanny Piggins did not normally approve of fruit, but in this instance the slightly overripe bananas provided a soft, if somewhat messy, landing. So Nanny Piggins

The baby, who was safe in her arms, smiled
delightedly, saying, "Again, again!"

slid down the barrow and landed on the pavement, with barely a hair out of place. The baby, who was safe in her arms, smiled delightedly, saying, "Again, again!"

"All right," said Nanny Piggins. She had enjoyed the fall too. She did not get to do much plummeting these days (since she'd left the circus). So Nanny Piggins was just about to climb back up the stairs to take another turn when everyone from the street (and it was a crowded street) rushed forward to praise her.

"You're a hero!" exclaimed an elderly woman.

"It's like you're a trained acrobat," said a doughnut salesman.

"Well, actually—" began Nanny Piggins.

"My baby, my baby, my baby!" screamed the baby's mother.

"Have a free banana!" said the banana salesman, finding the one unsquashed banana left on his barrow.

A television camera and microphone were shoved in her face. (The television crew just happened to be in the street doing a story on the extortionate price of woks when they had caught Nanny Piggins's daring rescue on tape.)

"Who are you? How did you do that? Are you some kind of roving superhero?" asked the journalist.

"Not at all," said Nanny Piggins. "I'm just the world's greatest flying pig."

★ ★ ★

That night the footage of Nanny Piggins saving the baby was on the news. It looked even more spectacular in slow motion. Each acrobatic maneuver was even more graceful, and Nanny Piggins's hair looked even more fabulous.

"Wow, you're a celebrity!" exclaimed Michael.

"Nanny Piggins has always been a celebrity," Boris reminded him.

"But now you're a celebrity all over again," said Michael.

"That is the difficult thing about having enormous talent," said Nanny Piggins. "It is hard to stay out of the public spotlight. But don't worry, I am not going to pursue that life again. Tomorrow there will be some other spectacular footage on the news, perhaps a tap-dancing

ferret or a scuba-diving badger, and the world will forget about me."

.... ★ ★ ★ ....

But Nanny Piggins was only partially right. A badger
did scuba dive off the coast of Vanuatu, but that did not
mean everyone had lost interest in her.

It was a rainy morning, so Nanny Piggins was just
helping the children set up a soccer field in the living
room using Mr. Green's crystal trophies as goalposts (he
won the trophies for being the runner-up in "The Best
Tax Lawyer of the Year" award. There were only two
tax lawyers in the local area, so he won this award year
after year, and there was no shortage of goalposts), when
they were interrupted by the sound of the doorbell.

"You don't think your father has set up a closed-circuit
TV system, and he can see what we are up to?" asked Nanny
Piggins, looking about the room for hidden cameras.

"I don't think Father wants to know what we are up
to," said Derrick. Which was true; Mr. Green did not
notice what was going on when he was right there in

the same room as them, so it would not make sense for him to start paying attention when he was not.

"You hide, and I'll answer the door, just in case it's the truancy officer," said Nanny Piggins.

"But it's a Saturday," Derrick pointed out.

"I doubt that would stop her," said Nanny Piggins. "If that woman could lock you up in school seven days a week, I'm sure she would."

Nanny Piggins bravely approached the front door. She picked up an umbrella, just in case it was the truancy officer and she needed to poke her. But as Nanny Piggins swung the door open it immediately became apparent that it was not the truancy officer. For a start the truancy officer was an unusually tall woman, and this visitor was closer to Nanny Piggins's own height. Also, the truancy officer was very neat and precise, with a pinched expression on her face as if she had just stepped on a thumbtack, whereas this woman was a mess. She had crooked, smudged glasses and a mass of dark, wavy hair sticking out in the most peculiar directions, and she looked slightly bewildered, as though she could not remember how she had gotten there.

"What do you want?" asked Nanny Piggins suspiciously.

"To talk to you, please," said the messy woman.

"We don't want to change our phone service provider," said Nanny Piggins guardedly.

"Oh no, I'm not a door-to-door salesperson," said the messy woman. "I'm an author."

"Aaah, that explains your clothes," said Nanny Piggins. For the author looked like she had been sleeping in her moth-eaten clothes for at least a week (a common trait among writers).

"Why do you want to talk to Nanny Piggins?" asked Derrick.

"Because I saw you save that baby on the news last night. You were amazing!" said the author. "You are by far the most glamorous, athletic pig I've ever seen. Please, you have to let me write your biography."

"Hmm," said Nanny Piggins. "You'd better come in and have a slice of cake."

Nanny Piggins, Boris, the children, and Jo (that was the author's name) sat around the kitchen table, eating cake and debating whether or not Nanny Piggins should allow the author to write a book about her.

"I don't want to become any more famous," said Nanny Piggins. "Being universally admired can be so draining."

"It's all right, nobody reads nonfiction books," said Boris.

"Yuck, they're the worst kind," agreed Michael.

"Yes, but when they make an international block-buster movie out of the book, then everybody will see that," argued Nanny Piggins. "Also, I can't be bothered doing the work. If I talked nonstop twenty-four hours a day every day, with no cake breaks, it would still take me months to tell you even half the exciting things I've done."

"But you owe it to history to make a record of your life," argued Jo the author.

"There's more than enough history already," said Nanny Piggins. "I don't want to create any more. History teachers will just try to stuff it into the already overcrowded heads of poor, unfortunate children."

"But your life story will be much more exciting than all those other historical things, like the rise and fall of the Austro-Hungarian Empire," countered Derrick. Derrick was currently studying nineteenth-century Central European history at school and often had to pinch his own leg to stay awake.

"True," agreed Nanny Piggins, "although the two stories have many similarities."

"Why don't we just take it day by day," said Jo. "You can start telling me about your life, I'll start writing it down, and we'll just see how we go."

"Hmm," said Nanny Piggins, as she thought it over.

"It is raining," pointed out Michael, "so it's not as if we can build a solar-powered helicopter like we planned."

"I don't know..." said Nanny Piggins.

Jo put her slice of cake down on the table. "That's okay, if you really don't want me to write a book about you, I'll be all right," she said. "I've heard about a flying armadillo in Mexico named Eduardo. I could go and write about him instead."

Nanny Piggins leaped to her feet. "That amateur! He doesn't deserve to have a book written about him! No, you're writing about me. That's that. As soon as we've finished our soccer game."

And so Nanny Piggins, Boris, the children, and Jo

played soccer for an hour. Jo was not very good at soccer, or indeed anything involving foot-eye coordination, but she tried. And it was an excellent game. They smashed nine of Mr. Green's trophies, which was good because you got double points for a goal when you smashed the goalpost, and triple points if you got both goalposts.

Then they adjourned to the living room so that Nanny Piggins could begin recounting her life story. (They needed a room with lots of floor space, so Nanny Piggins could act out the exciting parts.)

"Where would you like me to start?" asked Nanny Piggins.

"It's always best to start at the beginning, so why don't you tell me about your mother," suggested Jo as she took a tape player out of her handbag, turned it on, and placed it on the coffee table.

"All right," said Nanny Piggins. "Of course, Mother died when I was very young, but what I remember, I remember well. She was a wonderful woman and a great natural athlete, especially in the vicinity of food. Mother could have been a flying pig if her career as a chef had not held her back."

"She was a chef?" asked Samantha.

"Oh yes," said Nanny Piggins. "At one time she won an award for being the greatest chef in Paris."

"Wow!" said the children.

"She was the first pig to be awarded the honor. But she was fired from her chef's job shortly after that," said Nanny Piggins sadly, "for refusing to send any food out to the customers. She insisted on eating everything she made. The problem was she was so good at cooking, she could not resist her own food."

"What a remarkable woman," said Jo. "Tell us more."

"Have you heard about the time she jumped from a moving train into the backseat of a sports car going one hundred miles per hour in the opposite direction, because she caught a glimpse of the driver eating a particularly delicious-looking cinnamon doughnut?" asked Nanny Piggins.

"No, but I'd love to," urged Jo.

And so Nanny Piggins launched into the amazing tale of the late Mrs. Piggins's years as a traveling chef. Jo scribbled down notes and had to recharge the batteries in the recorder three times to keep track of it all.

By two o'clock in the morning, Nanny Piggins had

just gotten up to the time her mother leaped off a yacht that was passing through the Dardanelles because she caught a whiff of Turkish delight.[4] At this point, Nanny Piggins noticed that the children were struggling to keep their eyes open and Boris was snoring loudly, so she stopped in the middle of her tale. "Perhaps we should leave it there and pick up again tomorrow," said Nanny Piggins.

"Awwww," said the children. "We wanted to find out if your mother ever perfected her recipe for baklava."

"Of course she did," said Nanny Piggins. "She was a Piggins, wasn't she?"

"I don't suppose you have her recipe book?" asked Jo. "If you did, we could publish the recipes throughout the biography. It would be a lovely tribute to such a great chef whose cooking career was so tragically cut short."

"Oh, I could never publish Mother's recipes," said Nanny Piggins. "That would be dangerous. Humans have enough problems with obesity already. If reci-

---

[4]Turkish delight is a delicious rosewater-flavored gel served in cubes and covered in powdered sugar. It was invented by Bekir Effendi, who opened a candy store in Istanbul, Turkey, in 1776. You may have heard of it if you have read *The Lion, the Witch and the Wardrobe*. In that book, the wicked queen uses Turkish delight to bribe the children, who have not seen candy for years due to war rationing.

pes that delicious were openly available, the entire population would weigh fifty pounds more by the end of the month."

"But you do have the recipes?" asked Jo.

"Tut-tut," said Nanny Piggins. "You wouldn't ask a magician how he did his tricks."

"Yes, I would," said Jo.

"Why don't you stay the night?" suggested Nanny Piggins. "And we can pick up tomorrow with the story of how I was recruited by the circus."

And so they all went to bed. The children dreamed of an internationally renowned chef. Nanny Piggins dreamed of being a little piglet again playing with her mother. And Boris dreamed he was dancing with a giant stick of honeycomb, like he always did.

The next morning when the children came down for breakfast, they found Nanny Piggins sitting at the table, eating cake, and scribbling down notes.

"I've had lots of ideas for stories I can tell Jo," explained Nanny Piggins.

"Brilliant!" said the children. It was still raining outside, so they would enjoy another day of listening to thrilling tales and eating the relevant snacks. (Nanny Piggins believed in fixing snacks to coordinate with stories; cake to celebrate happy stories, cake to cheer you up when you heard sad stories, and cake to spit everywhere when you heard a really good joke in a funny story.)

"Where's Jo?" asked Nanny Piggins.

"I saw her go into the bathroom," said Samantha. "She said she would be down in a minute."

"Excellent," said Nanny Piggins. And so they all dug into breakfast, knowing they would need the energy for a full day of listening. But by the time they had finished their sixth helpings of chocolate-covered waffles, the author had still not emerged.

"That's odd," said Nanny Piggins. "She's been in the bathroom for forty-five minutes."

"Perhaps she is particular about her appearance, and it takes her a long time to get ready," said Samantha.

"You'd never think so to look at her," snorted Nanny Piggins. "No, it's much more likely she's reading a novel in the bath and she's gotten to a very good part, so she can't get out because she doesn't want to stop reading. We had better go and rescue her, in case the bathwater gets cold and she develops hypothermia."

So as soon as they had finished their seventh helpings, Nanny Piggins and the children trooped upstairs to check on Jo.

Nanny Piggins called through the door, "Are you all right in there?" Then she lifted her trotter to knock, but the door swung open.

"That's odd," said Nanny Piggins. She peeked around the edge of the door. There was no sign of the author. "She's gone!"

The children came in to see for themselves.

"What has happened?" asked Derrick.

"You don't suppose she got sucked down the drain?" asked Nanny Piggins, as she eyed the bathtub. She was secretly afraid of drain holes and always made sure she was out of the bath before she drained the water.

Samantha laid her hand on the side of the tub. "It's not wet. So she never even had a bath."

"Tut-tut," said Nanny Piggins. "Someone really

should take these authors in hand. It is bad enough they have terrible haircuts and awful clothes. But they should at least be made to wash."

"Perhaps something happened to her before she had a chance to bathe," said Derrick. "Look, the window is open."

The curtains were flapping in the breeze.

"What are you suggesting?" asked Nanny Piggins. "Who would dream of climbing up the outside of a house, going in through the bathroom window, and kidnapping a dirty author—?" Before Nanny Piggins had even finished her sentence, they all knew the answer.

"The Ringmaster!" they gasped in unison.

They rushed to the window and looked out. And sure enough, there, snagged on the drainpipe, was one of the lurid, fake-gold buttons the Ringmaster wore on his jacket.

"That poor woman," said Nanny Piggins. "As we speak she is probably being forced to write books in front of crowds of circus-goers."

"That doesn't sound very entertaining," said Derrick.

"The Ringmaster will think of some way to jazz it

up," said Nanny Piggins, "by making her write upside down on an elephant or something."

"What are we going to do?" asked Samantha.

"We'll just have to rescue her," said Nanny Piggins. "I seem to be rescuing a lot of people this week."

And so Nanny Piggins packed the children into Mr. Green's Rolls-Royce (after making Mr. Green walk to work), and they set off for the circus. Nanny Piggins had never taken the children to the circus before because she believed that coming within a five-hundred-yard radius of the Ringmaster was dangerous. Also, Nanny Piggins did not believe in looking back, and on some level she knew that going to the circus would make her sad. For while she did not miss the cold tents, the endless work-load, or the Ringmaster's tyrannical ways, somewhere deep down she did sometimes secretly miss the roar of the crowd. And Nanny Piggins feared that setting one foot inside the big top would make her want to go back.

But in this instance Nanny Piggins was prepared to

face her demons, because there was something more important at stake. She could not allow the Ringmaster to go around kidnapping authors. True, Jo was not an important author (she did not write romance novels), but it was the principle of the matter. Without authors, there would be no books. And without books, everyone would be forced to talk to the person sitting next to them on the train, and she just could not let that happen.

As soon as they caught their first glimpse of the big top through the windshield of the car, Derrick and Michael became excited. The huge colored tents and bright circus posters are designed to enthrall the imaginations of children. Only Samantha was concerned.

"It seems terribly cruel that the animals are forced to live in those cages," she worried.

"Don't worry; the doors aren't locked," said Boris.

"They're not?" yelped Samantha. This made her worry even more.

"Oh no, the Ringmaster is a tyrant, but he isn't rude," said Boris. "The cages are just for show to make the public feel safe. We only had to go and sit in them when the occupational health and safety man came around."

"But the circus animals never bite people, do they?" asked Samantha.

"Oh no," said Boris. "Not unless you get your cotton candy stuck in their fur. They don't like that."

"Okay," said Nanny Piggins. "I'll hide your father's Rolls-Royce behind that pile of elephant poo, or in front of it; it doesn't matter because they are the same color. Then we'll sneak over to the Ringmaster's caravan to see if the author is inside."

When they got to the Ringmaster's caravan all the windows were covered with curtains, so Boris lifted Michael up onto the roof so he could peek in through the skylight.

"What can you see?" asked Nanny Piggins.

"The Ringmaster's got a really impressive teaspoon collection," marveled Michael.

"Yes, it's his favorite hobby. He buys one in every town the circus goes to. But can you see the author?" asked Nanny Piggins.

"Hang on; I'll just twist around...yes! She's in there. He's tied her to a chair," said Michael.

"And what's the Ringmaster doing?" asked Nanny Piggins.

"He's standing in front of a mirror and twirling his mustache," said Michael.

"Of course, that's his second-favorite hobby," said Nanny Piggins.

"Do you want us to provide a diversion while you sneak the author out?" asked Derrick.

Nanny Piggins looked at her watch. "I don't think so. I'm hungry and it's time for second morning tea, so I don't want to mess around. Boris, would you mind terribly punching a huge hole in the wall?"

"Not at all," said Boris. He was always happy to help his sister. So he punched his fists through the wall of the Ringmaster's caravan, grabbed hold of the thin metal sheeting, and tore a huge piece off, allowing Nanny Piggins and the children to walk straight inside.

"Sarah Piggins, how wonderful to see you!" lied the Ringmaster, ignoring the irreparable damage done to his home.

The Ringmaster kissed Nanny Piggins loudly, first on one cheek and then the other, to which Nanny Piggins responded by stomping hard on his foot. This is the way they always greeted each other.

"You are a very naughty man!" condemned Nanny Piggins.

"And that's what you love about me," said the Ringmaster with no shame.

Nanny Piggins just rolled her eyes. "I cannot allow you to go around kidnapping authors. What were you thinking?"

"Yes, it's one thing to go around kidnapping circus performers," said Boris as he and the children untied the author. "We're professionals in the field, so we expect it. But you can't kidnap normal people. They have families and jobs, and they just don't like it."

"But, Sarah Piggins, you've only got yourself to blame," said the Ringmaster, wagging his finger at Nanny Piggins like she was a naughty schoolgirl. "You were the one who let her start work on your biography. Now obviously I can't allow that."

"Why not?" asked Derrick.

"I can't allow someone to write a book about what goes on in the circus," said the Ringmaster. "It would give away too many of our secrets."

"You mean you would spend too many years in jail if the police found out," said Boris.

"That too," admitted the Ringmaster.

At this point, Boris removed the gag from the author's mouth, and the whole argument became redundant.

"You stupid man," yelled the author.

Even the Ringmaster was taken aback. "She's a fiery one, isn't she?"

"I was never going to write a book about her!" Jo said, pointing at Nanny Piggins.

"You weren't?!" exclaimed everyone else.

"Of course not. I could barely stand listening to her never-ending stories," said the author. "I just wanted Mummy's recipe book."

"Mummy?" said Nanny Piggins, with which she stepped forward and whipped the glasses off the author's face.

Everyone gasped. Beneath the smudged glasses and messy hair was a stunningly beautiful pig, who looked exactly like Nanny Piggins.

"Why, it's Nadia Piggins, one of my identical fourteentuplet sisters!" exclaimed Nanny Piggins. "I thought you looked familiar."

"I've spent years searching for Mummy's recipe book.

I could make a fortune getting it published. I've tried Charlotte, Anthea, Beatrice, Abigail, Gretel, Deidre, Jeanette, Ursula, Sophia, Sue, Katerina, and Wendy, but none of them has it. So I knew it was with you!" said Nadia Piggins. "I was just about to sneak into your room and search for it when I was kidnapped."

"Why didn't you just ask?" said Nanny Piggins. "I could have told you that Mother's recipe book was destroyed years ago when it accidentally fell into a bowl of cake mix and she ate it."

"It's gone?" said Nadia Piggins, totally aghast.

"Gone forever," confirmed Nanny Piggins. "You remember how good her black forest chocolate cake was. A book covered in that never stood a chance."

"What am I going to do?" wailed Nadia. "I've spent my whole life looking for that recipe book."

"Why don't you spend the rest of your life making up recipes that are just as good?" suggested Nanny Piggins. "That is the wonderful thing about cooking. If you make something that tastes bad, you get to cook and eat it again and again until it's perfect. It's a win–win–win scenario. Or, rather, an eat–eat–eat scenario."

"Making up my own recipes? That's not a bad idea," conceded Nadia Piggins. "I'll enroll in chef school immediately."

"What a relief," said Nanny Piggins. "If you become a chef, you will have to wear a chef's hat and finally we won't have to look at your hair."

And so Nanny Piggins, Boris, and the children left the circus as quickly as possible, before Nanny Piggins could be tempted to blast herself out of a cannon for old times' sake. And before the Ringmaster could devise a way to kidnap any of them.

As they drove away, Derrick asked his nanny, "Are you sad that there won't be a book about you?"

"Not at all," said Nanny Piggins. "I don't think a book could ever do justice to the exciting things that happen to me on a daily basis. Not unless the pages were made out of chocolate."

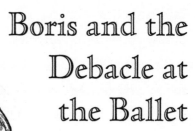

CHAPTER EIGHT

Boris and the Debacle at the Ballet

Shhhh, be very quiet. No sudden moves," whispered Nanny Piggins as she and the children crouched on the kitchen floor, staring in through the oven door. They were watching their chocolate soufflé.

"Now the heat will make the air we whipped into the mixture expand. At the same time, the egg will start to cook, causing it to lose its tertiary structure and solidify. And that is what holds the soufflé in its deliciously light and fluffy state," explained Nanny Piggins quietly.

"Wow! It's like science," whispered Michael.

"It is science," whispered back Nanny Piggins. "Only the science of cooking is much more important than that quantum physics or carbon chemistry stuff they obsess about at universities."

"It's starting to rise!" breathed Samantha excitedly as the soufflé slowly began to lift.

"Excellent!" whispered Nanny Piggins. "Now everyone be completely silent. The slightest vibration can cause the air to escape before the egg has cooked, which would make it flop like a pancake."

But just then—*BANG!*—the back door in the kitchen slammed open, and Boris (all thousand pounds plus of him) burst into the kitchen. "Have you seen this three-week-old newspaper?!!" he yelled.

Nanny Piggins and the children turned to look at Boris, then turned back to look at their soufflé, just in time to see it collapse back into the bottom of the dish.

"Awww," groaned the children.

"What?" asked Boris.

"We were making a soufflé," explained Nanny Piggins.

"I thought you were going to get a red, flashing light installed to warn me when delicate things were being cooked," said Boris. "I would have waited until the egg lost its tertiary structure if I'd known."

"Yes, but if I knew there were going to be no loud bangs to ruin my soufflé then there would be no risk, and that would take the thrill out of it," said Nanny Piggins. "Now, what are you so excited about?"

"My old ballet company, the Russian Ballet, is coming here to perform *Swan Lake* this week!" exclaimed Boris. "We've got to get tickets! May I borrow Mr. Green's credit card?"

"Of course," said Nanny Piggins as she fished the card out of her shoe. (She kept the real one there. The card in Mr. Green's wallet was a fake made out of papier-mâché. Fortunately he was too cheap to pay for anything, so he never realized.) "An evening at the ballet is an educational experience. I'm sure Mr. Green would be happy to pay for it, if he was anybody other than himself and therefore a reasonable person."

"But can't you ask one of your friends in the ballet company to give you free tickets?" asked Derrick.

At this point Boris looked sheepish. He even blushed, although you could not tell, because his red face was covered by brown fur. "Oh, I couldn't do that," said Boris.

"Why not?" asked Samantha.

"You were their star for years," said Michael. "I'm sure they'd be delighted to see you."

"Oh, I'm sure *they* would, but I'd be embarrassed," said Boris.

"Why?" asked Michael. He could understand someone being embarrassed for forgetting to take off their pajamas before going to school, or for accidentally putting their shirt on inside out and back-to-front (before Nanny Piggins had arrived and taken control of his wardrobe, Michael had done things like that all the time). But since Boris was a bear and did not wear clothes, Michael did not understand what he could possibly be embarrassed about.

"All my old friends from the ballet are still proud professional dancers," said Boris, "whereas I . . . well . . . I've let myself go. I don't do anything anymore."

"What are you talking about?" protested Nanny Piggins. "You are the busiest bear I know! Just yesterday you helped me fetch the newspaper the delivery boy managed to hurl up into Mrs. McGill's tree."

"And you helped me make a diorama of an alien space station that fires real space goo," added Michael.

"And you teach yoga to homeless people in the park," added Derrick. "Even the ones who don't want to learn."

"And you're better at hugging than anybody I know," added Samantha.

"Yes, I *do* do all that. But it isn't dancing, is it?" said Boris. "I used to be the best ballet-dancing bear in the entire world. And now..." His bottom lip began to quiver. "I'm just a bear."

"But you're always dancing around the garden," said Derrick. "That ballet you did yesterday to express how sad you felt when the lawn mower wouldn't start was really beautiful."

Boris blushed again. "It's very kind of you to say that, but I don't think the dancers at the Russian Ballet will see it that way. You see, dancers enjoy being mean to each other. It makes them feel less bad about themselves."

"They wouldn't be so mean if they weren't half starved on crazy diets all the time," muttered Nanny Piggins.

"You're probably right," agreed Boris. "The year they all went on the Israeli Army Diet was unbearable. You

185

could never go to the toilet because there was always someone in there crying."

"Are you sure they're your friends, then?" asked Samantha.

"Oh yes, they're my very dear friends. It's traditional for ballet dancers to be horrible to each other. If dancers aren't horrible to you, you know they've got no respect for your footwork," explained Boris. "So I do want to see all my old friends. But since I'd rather not talk to them, I'd better just pay for the tickets."

That night they all got dressed to go to the ballet. Nanny Piggins insisted they dress appropriately, which meant white tie and tailcoats for the boys and ball gowns and long gloves for herself and Samantha. It was hard to find a tailcoat that fit Boris off the rack, and the tuxedo rental shop refused to rent one to him when they found out he was a bear (despite Nanny Piggins's threats to sue them for species-ism).

Fortunately, Nanny Piggins was able to whip up a tailcoat and pants herself, by cutting up the curtains from Mr. Green's bedroom and dyeing them black, then making a white shirt, vest, and bow tie out of Mr. Green's bed sheets. So when they finally headed into town, they were by far the most stylish people on the bus.

As they entered the theater lobby, the children were immediately impressed. It was a very grand building. There were lots of marble columns, gold-colored decorations, statues of armless women, and furniture upholstered with red velvet. "How does it feel to be back in a ballet theater?" asked Samantha.

"Like coming home," sobbed Boris, completely breaking down. He had to give them each several bear hugs to cheer himself back up. Then the five-minute bell rang, so they all went into the theater to find their seats.

"You don't think anyone will recognize me, do you?" asked Boris as he put on a pair of sunglasses to try to hide his identity.

"Oh no, not at all," lied Derrick kindly. Boris was gifted at transforming himself into whatever he portrayed, but at the end of the day he was a ten-foot-tall, thousand-pound-plus bear and, therefore, he did tend to catch the eye.

The usher showed them to their seats. Nanny Piggins and the children sat down. But Boris just looked at his seat, his lip quivering. "I don't think my bottom is going to fit in that gap," said Boris as tears welled in his eyes.

Nanny Piggins had only brought three boxes of tissues with her, so she sought to stem the flow. "The carpenter has obviously made a dreadful mistake," said Nanny Piggins kindly. "That seat is much smaller than any other one in the theater. But it's all right; Michael will share his seat with you. Then you can have two seats so you can spread out and be comfortable. Michael, you don't mind sitting on Boris, do you?"

"Not at all," said Michael.

At that moment, the lights went down, and everyone in the hall hushed (except the person sitting behind Boris, who wept quietly, knowing that she was not going to see a single moment of the ballet sitting behind a ten-foot-tall bear with a little boy perched on his head).

The introductory overture started and, as the music swelled, Prince Siegfried danced onto the stage in pursuit of a flock of swans. Soon, through the magic of music and movement, the audience was transported back in time to the fantasy land of Russian folktales, making everyone believe that they really were in the Siberian forest, that tights really were a normal thing to wear when you were out hunting, and that all those skinny women dancers really were beautiful swans.

Next, Princess Odette danced out onto the stage. The already spellbound crowd was awed by her beauty. She paused to acknowledge the applause, then skipped lightly to the front of the stage, where she leaped high in the air and spun in a beautiful triple pirouette before suddenly and unexpectedly disappearing from sight as she missed the stage completely and crashed down into the orchestra pit.

"Aaaaggghhh!" screamed the ballet dancer playing Odette.

"Ow!" said the viola player she landed on.

Odette then loudly screamed several rude words. Fortunately, no one in the audience except Boris and Nanny Piggins could understand Russian, so it did not matter, although Nanny Piggins held her trotters over Michael's ears just in case.

The stage manager and the ballet company's physical therapist rushed to help the stricken ballerina. Boris could distinctly hear the Russian words for "broken ankle" and "don't be silly, of course you can't dance with a broken ankle," emerging from the pit.

"What's happening?" asked Samantha.

"I think they're going to have to cancel the performance," said Boris.

"Won't there be an understudy?" asked Derrick.

"Oh no, there's never an understudy," said Boris. "Principal ballerinas always feel threatened by their understudies, so they usually push them down a flight of stairs or poison them before they go on tour."

The stage manager got up onstage and gestured for silence. "Please," he said, addressing the entire audience. "Is there anybody in the theater who is a ballet master and knows the role of Odette?"

The audience muttered among themselves and looked about to see if anyone was going to stand up. No one did except Nanny Piggins, but Derrick grabbed her by the arm. "Sit down, Nanny Piggins; you aren't a ballet master."

"How do I know until I try?" protested Nanny Piggins.

But then Boris removed Michael from his head and proudly rose to his feet.

"I, Boris the bear, know the role of Odette," announced Boris. (Back when he was a ballet dancer, Boris had normally played Prince Siegfried, because that is the boy's part. But if you hold a woman up above your head often enough you come to know her well, so Boris was familiar with the woman's part too.)

The dancers onstage were amazed and muttered among themselves in Russian. "Look who it is!" "It's Boris, the greatest ballet-dancing bear in the world!" "Doesn't he look dashing in that tailcoat?"

The audience watched in stunned silence as Boris made his way to the front of the theater and climbed up onto the stage, only stopping to peer into the orchestra pit and speak to the stricken ballerina. "Hello, Svetlana, I'm terribly sorry about your ankle. But don't worry; I'll fill in. I'll play Odette just the way you do, so if anyone is late they won't even notice I'm not you."

Boris was then ushered backstage. He reappeared

moments later in a white tutu. The children did not recognize him at first because he moved with all the beauty and grace of a ballerina. But there were a few distinctive characteristics—his movements were even more graceful and beautiful than the other dancers, plus if you looked closely you could see that he was still ten feet tall and covered in fur.

The ballet resumed, and it was wonderful. Nanny Piggins got so caught up in the story that the children had to restrain her several times from running up onstage and telling off the wicked Baron Von Rothbart. Then at the end, when Odette and Siegfried jumped into the lake and Nanny Piggins realized that they were not just going swimming, she was devastated. They were all very glad Nanny Piggins had brought three boxes of tissues. They had never seen a pig cry so hard.

Boris's portrayal of Odette had been perfect. It was the best performance of *Swan Lake* ever. True, the dancer playing Siegfried had struggled to lift Boris, but Boris just lifted him instead. And nobody, except a ballet aficionado, would ever notice the difference.

As the curtain closed and the audience burst into

applause, Nanny Piggins and the children climbed up on their seats to clap and whistle the loudest. Boris had to come back out and bow seventeen times before the theater management got tired of it and started flashing the lights on and off to make everybody go home.

"Come along," said Nanny Piggins. "Let's go backstage and tell Boris how wonderful he was."

Backstage, it was hard to get to Boris's dressing room because so many people had crowded around to congratulate him. There were ballet dancers and orchestra players and rich people with nothing better to do everywhere, and they were all babbling in Russian. Eventually Nanny Piggins made her way to the front by saying "izvinitye" (Russian for "excuse me") and, when that did not work, by stomping on a few feet.

They found Boris reclining in his dressing room, wearing a purple silk robe and sipping honey tea while a gaggle of adoring ballet critics, theater management, and other important people gathered around him.

"Boris, you were magnificent," praised Nanny Piggins.

"I never knew *Swan Lake* was so awesome," said Derrick.

"It was even better than that ballet you did to show Headmaster Pimplestock what you thought of his curriculum," added Michael.

Samantha did not say anything. She just hugged Boris's leg with pride.

"Thank you, darlings; it did go well, didn't it?" said Boris.

"Let's go home and create a dessert to name after you," suggested Nanny Piggins. "I'm sure we can come up with something better than the pavlova they named after that hack what's-her-name."

"I wish I could. But Mikhail has asked me to join the company for a pot of honey back at their hotel," said Boris, nodding toward the dancer who had played Siegfried. "I'd invite you along, but it would be boring for you listening to a bunch of old dancers reminisce."

Mikhail and Svetlana (who was sitting there with her leg propped up on a bag of ice) laughed.

"Oh," said Nanny Piggins.

"Don't wait up for me," said Boris as he turned back and started talking to Mikhail and Svetlana in Russian.

Nanny Piggins led the children away.

"Is Boris all right?" asked Samantha. "He seems to be acting peculiarly."

"Performers are often a little strange after a show," explained Nanny Piggins. "It's because the fear and the adrenaline haven't worn off yet. Don't worry; I'm sure he'll be back to normal tomorrow."

"I hope so," said Michael. "Boris the ballet star doesn't seem as nice as Boris the bear who lives in the shed."

The next morning, Nanny Piggins and the children were, again, crouched on the kitchen floor, staring in through the oven door as they watched their second attempt at chocolate soufflé. There was no whispering this time—just to be sure. If they wanted to communicate with one another they wrote notes, very quietly, on a notepad.

"It smells delicious," wrote Samantha.

"That is a good sign," Nanny Piggins wrote back.

"Smell is a sure indicator of cooking. This is the crucial stage—everyone try to breathe quietly."

The children took small, shallow breaths as instructed, and the soufflé gradually started to lift... when—*BANG!*—the back door slammed open.

"Good morning," called Boris as he did a grand jeté (a flying leap) into the room. The moment he landed, the soufflé sank, along with the culinary hopes of Nanny Piggins and the children.

They turned to look at Boris. He was still wearing his tailcoat, although the white bow tie hung loose, and he was carrying four dozen red roses in one arm with a huge bucket of half-eaten honey in the other.

"Did you have a good night?" asked Nanny Piggins politely.

"Oh, Sarah, it was marvelous," gushed Boris. "And the most wonderful thing has happened. They have offered me my old job back, as the male lead in their new ballet. They did offer me principal ballerina because I was so much better than Svetlana at playing Odette. But I think I would prefer to play the male roles. I don't want to be typecast."

"But you aren't going to take the job, are you?" asked Michael.

"Why wouldn't I?" replied Boris.

"Because the Russian Ballet Company is based in Russia. It's going to take forever for you to travel back and forth to Russia every day," said Michael.

The others looked at Michael. It was times like this that they remembered that he was the youngest and most naive.

Boris just laughed. "You silly billy. I will, of course, be moving back to my homeland, Mother Russia."

Michael burst into tears and ran out of the room.

"What's wrong with him?" asked Boris.

"He's just had his feelings hurt by a very stupid bear," said Nanny Piggins sternly.

"He'll get over it," said Boris as he got up to return to his shed. "And you must all come and visit me in Moscow, after a year or two when I have settled in." With that, Boris left the same way he entered—banging the back door loudly.

"What on earth has happened to Boris?" asked Samantha.

"He is suffering from a tragic medical condition," said Nanny Piggins. "His head has become swollen. It is a very common malady in the entertainment industry. It can strike anyone, even lovely, caring bears."

Boris just laughed. "You silly billy. I will, of course, be moving back to my homeland, Mother Russia."

"What can we do?" asked Derrick.

"Make another soufflé," said Nanny Piggins.

"How will that help?" asked Samantha.

"It will give us something to eat while we wait for him to come to his senses," explained Nanny Piggins.

The next three days were long and wearisome for Nanny Piggins and the children, because Boris's behavior only grew more and more obnoxious. He had taken to eating caviar, laughing loudly at things that were not funny, and looking at himself doing ballet moves in the mirror all the time.

On the third day, when Nanny Piggins had just put another soufflé in the oven and it had just been ruined, again, this time by the phone ringing loudly at the crucial moment—it was the doorman from the ballet theater calling to say that Boris would not be coming home for dinner—Nanny Piggins decided she'd had enough.

"What are you going to do?" asked Derrick.

"I am going to give my brother a piece of my mind," said Nanny Piggins. "Come along."

"You want us to come with you?" asked Samantha. She was used to adults preferring to yell at one another behind closed doors, while pretending that the doors were entirely soundproof.

"I will need witnesses if things turn violent," explained Nanny Piggins. "And bring along the ruined soufflé as evidence to show how sorely I was provoked."

And so they went to the theater, Nanny Piggins muttering all the way as she practiced all the really cutting things she was going to say to Boris.

When they arrived at the theater building, Nanny Piggins did not hesitate. There was a stage door around the side where they could easily be let in. But Nanny Piggins preferred to kick in the main doors at the front. (If you are going to tell someone off, it always helps to make a dramatic entrance first.) And so they burst into the theater foyer.

But it was not the people inside who were shocked and surprised. The shocked and surprised ones were Nanny Piggins and the children, for they had just burst in on Svetlana and Mikhail as they danced about the room (to loud music, which is why they had not noticed Nanny Piggins's dramatic entrance). They saw Mikhail pick Svetlana up and throw her in the air, where she spun around three times before landing on what was supposed to be her injured foot.

Nanny Piggins went over to the stereo and switched it off. Mikhail's and Svetlana's heads whipped around.

"Either your broken ankle has healed quicker than any broken ankle in the history of broken ankles, or there is something fishy going on here," said Nanny Piggins.

Svetlana sat down quickly and clutched her foot. "The pain, it comes and goes."

"You might be a world-famous ballerina, but you are not a very good actress," said Nanny Piggins. "You are clutching the wrong foot."

Svetlana hastily clutched both feet.

"We don't have to explain ourselves to a common pig," said Mikhail, puffing out his chest.

"Really?" said Nanny Piggins, her eyes narrowing.

"You're going to regret saying that," warned Derrick.

"Michael, run and fetch Boris," said Nanny Piggins.

Michael rushed off.

"I'm leaving," said Svetlana.

Nanny Piggins blocked her path. "Don't for one moment think that the fact that I am wearing a vintage designer outfit (which looks really lovely) will stop me from wrestling you to the ground and holding you in a body lock," said Nanny Piggins.

Svetlana looked at Nanny Piggins. Nanny Piggins glowered back. And Svetlana decided today was not the day she would try pig wrestling.

Just then Michael reentered, dragging Boris.

"This had better be good," said Boris. "The choreographer gets cross if I miss practice."

"Boris, I have reason to believe you have been hoodwinked," said Nanny Piggins. "Svetlana's ankle is not really broken!"

"But that's good news, isn't it?" said Boris.

"What?" said Nanny Piggins.

"If someone thought their ankle was broken and then it turned out it wasn't, you've got to be happy about that," said Boris.

"But the question is—why was she pretending it was broken?" asked Nanny Piggins.

"You've been reading too many historical romance novels again, haven't you?" said Boris as he patronizingly patted his sister on the head.

Nanny Piggins began to shake with rage. For the first

time since she had adopted him, Nanny Piggins was actually considering biting her own brother on the leg.

"Why would anyone want to pretend to have a broken ankle?" continued Boris.

Just then a caretaker entered the lobby carrying an armful of rolled-up bill posters. "Is it all right if I start putting up the new posters?" he asked.

"*Nyet!*" screamed Mikhail and Svetlana (which is Russian for "No!"). Mikhail actually lunged forward to try to grab the posters away, but Nanny Piggins was too quick for him. When it comes to lunging, no one lunges like a flying pig. She threw herself at the caretaker and his posters with the speed and precision of a heat-seeking missile.

"Why don't you want us to see this?" asked Nanny Piggins as she unfurled the rolled-up posters. The children gathered around to look at it over their nanny's shoulder. The poster was an advertisement for a new show the Russian Ballet Company would perform when they returned to Russia. It was called *The Ballet of Baris the Dancing Buffoon*. The poster showed a large bear, dressed as a clown and lumbering about as a group of beautiful skinny people laughed at him.

Boris gasped. "*Nyet!*" he exclaimed.

"*Da*," said Nanny Piggins (which is Russian for "yes").

"You told me if I came back to Russia with you, I would get to dance Romeo in *Romeo and Juliet*," said Boris.

Mikhail snorted (which is Russian for contemptuous laughter). "As if we would let a bear play such a great and important role. No, we have to stage this new ballet to get government funding. But none of us wanted to play the buffoon."

"Then we think of Boris the bear," said Svetlana. "For you, this role is perfect."

"You mean this whole thing, the broken ankle and letting me dance Odette, was all a trick?" said Boris.

"Of course it was," snapped Mikhail. "We only toured here so we could lure you back. We couldn't believe it when you did not buy tickets to the show."

"We had to break into your shed and put a three-week-old newspaper in there," added Svetlana. "I almost broke my ankle for real climbing in through the window."

"Wow! That was a really elaborate trick," said Michael, struggling not to be impressed.

Boris looked at the poster. "So you only want me so I can dance like a buffoon?"

"Of course. You are perfect for the role," said Svetlana. "The crowds would flock to see you lumber about like a giant idiot."

Boris drew himself up to his full height (ten and a half feet when he stood up straight) so his head brushed the theater's huge chandelier. "I, Boris the bear, am the greatest ballet-dancing bear in the world. It is you who are the fools, for spurning my superior talent and trying to make a mockery of me. I spit on your job offer."

"Boris," chided Nanny Piggins.

"At least I would, if spitting weren't vulgar," added Boris. "You can go back to Russia and play your own buffoon. Farewell forever!"

With that, Boris spun on his heel and strode dramatically out of the theater.

Nanny Piggins glowered at Mikhail and Svetlana. "Samantha, do you still have that notepad?"

"Yes," said Samantha, taking the soufflé notepad and pencil from her pocket.

"Write this down: 'Note to self—get revenge on the Russian Ballet Company,'" dictated Nanny Piggins.

"Got it," said Samantha as she wrote down every word.

"And be sure to stick that on the refrigerator when we get home so I don't forget," added Nanny Piggins.

Then she and the children left in search of Boris. They found him sitting on the curb, crying.

"There, there, you'll get another dancing job," Nanny Piggins assured him. "You are the best dancing bear in the world."

"You're the best dancing *anything* in the world," said Michael.

"Everyone loved your Odette," Samantha reminded him.

"When they hear that you have come out of retirement, all the ballet companies will want you," assured Derrick.

"That's not why I'm crying," sobbed Boris. "I know I am a much better dancer than those double-left-footed idiots. I'm crying because I've been such a bad brother and friend. Can you ever forgive me?" He grabbed Nanny Piggins and the children in such a tight bear hug it was several minutes before they had enough air in their lungs to assure him he was entirely forgiven.

"But aren't you sorry to leave the ballet theater behind?" asked Samantha.

"Well, I do like some parts, like starring in the show, throwing the other dancers high in the air, and everyone in the audience cheering and clapping. But I'd forgotten about all the bad parts," confessed Boris.

"What bad parts?" asked Michael.

"You have to practice every single day. Even on days when your toes are tired," said Boris.

"How awful," sympathized Michael.

"And they don't let you sleep peacefully in your shed until two in the afternoon," said Boris. "They make you get up early in the morning. Sometimes as early as ten AM!"

"That's ridiculous," said Nanny Piggins. "You need your rest; you're a growing bear."

"But that's not the worst part." Boris started to tear up again.

"You can tell us, Boris," said Samantha, gently patting his paw.

"They made me go on a diet!" he wailed, before completely breaking down into wracking sobs. It was hard to understand what he said next because he was weeping so loudly, but it was something like, "They said I weighed nine hundred pounds more than a normal ballet dancer."

"You poor, poor bear," said Nanny Piggins, hugging him tightly. "We rescued you not a moment too soon. Come along; we will take you home. And if you promise to cry quietly in another room while we make it, we will give you a slice of The Boris."

"You named a dessert after me?" asked Boris, cheering up immediately. "What is it? A cake? A steamed pudding? Something meringue-based?"

"No, The Boris is a chocolate and honey soufflé!" announced Nanny Piggins.

"With a great big piece of honeycomb stuck in the middle," added Michael. "That part was my idea."

Nanny Piggins hugged Michael proudly. "Not since Mozart has one so young created something so beautiful. Now let's go home and whip up a few dozen Borises so we can all have lots and lots for lunch."

And things in the Green household soon returned to normal. With one exception. While he did not want to be an international ballet superstar, Boris did still love to dance. So Nanny Piggins introduced him to the old lady who ran the local ballet school, and she gave him a job teaching a preschool ballet class on Saturday mornings. The little girls and boys loved Boris because he was such a great teacher. And he loved choreograph-ing little ballets for them—about the delight of eating cotton candy, the fun of making mud pies, and the joy of having a sister who makes delicious soufflé. All of which were far better than that very silly story about a tights-wearing hunter and a depressed swan.

CHAPTER NINE

Nanny Piggins and the Cake Stall

At the back of the school hall, Boris was fast asleep and snoring loudly while Nanny Piggins and the children avidly read a thrilling vampire novel. They read it in an unusual way. After Nanny Piggins finished a page she would tear it out and hand it to Derrick, who read it and handed it to Samantha, who read it and handed it to Michael. They often enjoyed books this way—they found it saved arguments (and the subsequent wrestling matches) over who was going to read the book first. And this is how they always whiled away the time when they went to the school's monthly PTA meetings. Nanny Piggins did not believe in listening to all the boring things that Headmaster Pimplestock blathered on about. She was just waiting for the good part, when the chairman would ask, "Any other business?"

This was when Nanny Piggins would leap to her trotters and start giving the parents and teachers a piece of her mind. The subject of her ranting was always the same—school uniforms. She would begin by denouncing the concept generally, then go on to specifically list every one of the design faults in both the boys' and girls' uniforms.

The PTA had heard this speech many times before. They even mouthed along with the words in the good bits. They all enjoyed the part where Nanny Piggins pointed her trotter at Headmaster Pimplestock and accused him of being an alien from a distant galaxy who had come to Earth and abducted the real headmaster's body just so he could inflict his own terrible taste in clothes on the citizens of this planet. When Nanny Piggins finished and sat down, everyone clapped. Her speeches were the only interesting thing ever to happen at the PTA meetings (if you don't count the great pizza versus lentil burgers debate of 1972).

"Please, Nanny Piggins," pleaded Headmaster Pimplestock. "I have told you time and time again, the school just does not have the money to fly in a leading Italian designer to overhaul the school uniform."

"Well, what are you wasting the school fees on?" demanded Nanny Piggins. "I've seen the checks Mr. Green writes out to you, and they are enormous!" (They were not enormous at all. Mr. Green had enrolled his children in the cheapest private school he could find, because he wanted the status of having privately educated children without actually having to bear the cost. But you have to understand, Nanny Piggins only earned ten cents an hour, so to her, any figure above three digits was huge.)

"The fees pay for books, electricity, and building maintenance," said Headmaster Pimplestock.

"Pish!" said Nanny Piggins. "I've seen how many chocolate cookies you have with your morning tea. I know how you really spend it."

The crowd giggled. Headmaster Pimplestock was a little tubby. He went bright red in the face. "Perhaps we should move on to the next item on the agenda. The school carnival is coming up. Who is going to volunteer to run a stall?" he asked, frantically trying to change the subject.

Nanny Piggins leaped to her feet again. "The carnival is a fund-raising event, isn't it?"

"Yes," said Headmaster Pimplestock warily.

"Then why can't that money be used to fly in the Italian designer?" asked Nanny Piggins.

"Because we need that money to repair the hole in the library roof you made when you fired yourself out of a cannon during book week," Headmaster Pimplestock said accusingly.

"Oh," said Nanny Piggins. (She could not deny she had made a rather large hole.) "But the children did learn a lot about physics from my demonstration."

"Ballistics is not the type of physics we want them to learn here," said Headmaster Pimplestock crushingly.

"Which is why so many of them fall asleep in class," muttered Nanny Piggins. (No one ever fell asleep during one of her cannon demonstrations, not unless they got hit on the head by a falling roof tile.)

"So as I was saying, the school carnival—" began Headmaster Pimplestock.

"Wait a moment," said Nanny Piggins as she rubbed her snout in concentration. "If the carnival makes more than enough money to fix the roof, can we use the extra money to hire the designer?"

Headmaster Pimplestock just laughed. "The estimate for the roof repair is $50,000, and given that the school fete has never raised more than $6,000, I don't think that is going to happen."

"But if we do, can we?" pressed Nanny Piggins.

"Sure, why not," said Headmaster Pimplestock, anxiously wanting Nanny Piggins to take her vampire novel and go home. "If we raise more than $50,000, then I promise to hire the greatest fashion designer in all of Milan to fly in on Monday."

"Excellent!" exclaimed Nanny Piggins. "Then I volunteer to run the cake stall."

At this point everyone burst out laughing.

Now, Nanny Piggins enjoyed a joke as much as the next pig, but she did not like being laughed at. (Nobody does, not even clowns, which is why they cry themselves to sleep every night.) Nanny Piggins particularly did not like it when a whole hall full of people laughed at her and she did not understand why.

"What?" she demanded.

"Nanny Anne runs the cake stall," explained Head-master Pimplestock. "She always does. It is the most successful part of the carnival."

Nanny Piggins scowled across the hall at Nanny Anne. Nanny Anne was her nemesis. She had perfect hair, perfect manners, and perfect etiquette, which made Nanny Piggins want to be sick. Right at that very moment Nanny Anne was sitting in her chair with perfect posture, as if the school had not bought three hundred of the most uncomfortable plastic chairs ever made. Everyone else in the room slouched, slumped, leaned, or teetered on their seats, desperately trying to find a half-comfortable position. But not Nanny Anne. She sat perfectly upright and still, because Nanny Anne thought it was much more important to be perfect than to be comfortable.

"Last year Nanny Anne made $7,000," praised Head-master Pimplestock.

Nanny Anne smiled.

"I thought you said the fete had never made more than $6,000?" said Nanny Piggins.

"The apple-bobbing stand ran at a loss after Mrs.

Arjuana got giddy and ran off to Vanuatu with the cash box," explained Headmaster Pimplestock.

It was Mrs. Arjuana's turn to blush.

"That was money well spent as far as I'm concerned," said Nanny Piggins. "I've seen your vacation snaps, Mrs. Arjuana, and you obviously had a lovely time."

Mrs. Arjuana smiled at Nanny Piggins.

Headmaster Pimplestock sought to move the meeting along. "If you want to be involved, Nanny Piggins, why don't I put you down for the bookstall, since you so clearly enjoy reading?"

Everyone in the hall snickered. They all knew Nanny Piggins spent every meeting reading thrilling novels. In fact, when the novel was particularly good, Nanny Piggins got Michael to keep passing the pages on around the whole room, so that everyone could enjoy them. (They'd had a wonderful evening the time Nanny Piggins brought in *The Adventure of the Speckled Band*. Absolutely no school business had been accomplished at all.)

"Books?" said Nanny Piggins. "Haven't you got anything more exciting? A catapult stand? A rat-catching demonstration? Fire-breathing lessons?"

"I can offer you books or knitwear," said Headmaster Pimplestock smugly. He so rarely got the better of Nanny Piggins and was enjoying himself, which was very silly because, as you have undoubtedly noticed, Nanny Piggins did have an amazing talent for getting retribution.

"All right, I'll take books," sulked Nanny Piggins.

"Good. Then meeting adjourned!" announced Headmaster Pimplestock, beating the table with a gavel and sprinting to his car before any of the parents (or nannies) could confront him, or notice how many packages of chocolate cookies he had in the backseat.

Nanny Piggins and the children were just gathering up all the loose pages of their vampire novel when Nanny Anne approached.

"Nanny Piggins, so good to see you," lied Nanny Anne with a saccharine smile.

"Nanny Anne," said Nanny Piggins as she scowled back. "I see you haven't been fired yet."

"I'm so glad you're going to run the little bookstall this year," said Nanny Anne. "If you need any pointers on how to handle a stall, just let me know. I have won Best Stallholder at the school fete for the last seven years."

"But surely Samson has only been going to this school for five years?" queried Nanny Piggins.

"I know, but I wanted to get involved in the school community early. It is so important to be a joiner," said Nanny Anne.

"Well, selling books is hardly rocket science. And since I know more than most rocket scientists, I think I can handle a bookstall," said Nanny Piggins.

"Yes, you would think so, but a nanny has to know her limitations," said Nanny Anne with false concern. "If it is too much for you, you mustn't be afraid to ask for help." Nanny Anne smiled her fake smile and walked away.

"I knew I should have worn my wrestling leotard to the PTA meeting," growled Nanny Piggins. "Samantha, hold my handbag. I'm going to crash-tackle her."

Samantha grabbed her nanny's trotter instead. "You'd better not. You know Nanny Anne always makes you pay her dry-cleaning bills when you attack her. Besides, Derrick needs help waking up Boris. We think he's fallen into one of his super-deep hibernation sleeps again."

And so, after Nanny Piggins had awoken her brother

by blasting him in the face with a fire extinguisher,[5] they all went home. On the way, Nanny Piggins tried to work out how they could earn over $50,000 at a bookstall.

"You could try to get hold of some really valuable books," suggested Derrick.

"What? You mean romance novels?" asked Nanny Piggins. These were her own personal favorite kind of books, and so she naturally assumed other people must value them as much as she did.

"No, the really valuable books are rare, old ones," said Samantha.

"Old books! Yuck!" said Nanny Piggins. "They always smell of dust and mold. And you never know who's been reading them, or whether they washed their

---

[5] Dear Reader, please don't think Nanny Piggins is cruel for blasting her brother in the face with a fire extinguisher. Nothing could be further from the truth. The fact is that it is incredibly difficult to wake up a fully grown Kodiak bear who has slipped into a super-deep hibernation sleep. So Boris doesn't mind at all when his sister sprays him with fire-retardant foam. In fact, the first time Nanny Piggins did it was when Boris fell asleep on a birthday cake, and his eyebrows caught fire from the candle flame. Boris was very grateful that his sister took such immediate action; apart from waking him up, she also saved his eyebrows, which are so vitally important for making facial expressions such as glowering and looking astonished.

hands before they turned the page. I don't believe any-body would pay a lot of money for tatty old books."

"They would," said Derrick. "A Gutenberg Bible is worth millions and millions of dollars."

"You're pulling my trotter!" said Nanny Piggins skeptically. "Millions of dollars? But there's a copy of the Bible in every hotel room in the world. And people give them away free at railway stations."

"But a Gutenberg Bible is the oldest book ever printed. There are only twenty-one perfect copies left in the world. That's why they're so valuable," explained Derrick. (He had learned this by watching a gripping mystery movie where someone was murdered for his Gutenberg Bible.)

"Really?" said Nanny Piggins. "Then let's hope someone has donated one to the bookstall."

The next morning, they were awoken by the delivery of the books (at what Nanny Piggins considered to be an obscenely early hour for a Saturday morning—10 AM). Throughout the year, parents, students, and good

Samaritans were able to drop off books in anticipation of the annual school fete. The only problem was that nobody ever donates their good books to a bookstall. They keep those for their own bookshelves. They only donate their awful books—the ones they are forced to read at school, the ones relatives buy for them as Christmas presents, and the ones they bought at the previous year's bookstall because they felt they just had to buy something. So when Nanny Piggins and the children opened the boxes, they were bitterly disappointed.

"Pee-yew! These books stink of dust! Can anyone see a Gutenberg Bible?" asked Nanny Piggins optimistically.

"No," said the children.

"I've found a set of the *Encyclopedia Britannica*," said Samantha.

"Well, that's good," said Nanny Piggins.

"Except the 'C' volume is missing," added Samantha.

"Nobody would want to buy a set of encyclopedias with 'C' missing. That's the best volume. The one with all the references to cannons, cakes, and chocolate," said Nanny Piggins.

"I've got a box full of phrase books," called out Michael.

"Well, that would be handy to anyone planning to go on vacation," said Nanny Piggins.

"Except none of them is in English," explained Michael. "There's Swahili to Thai, Russian to Esperanto, and Czech to Samoan…"

"And I've got a box full of knitting patterns," said Derrick.

"Well…" said Nanny Piggins, but then she gave up. Not even she could put a positive spin on knitting patterns. "Children, I am a brilliant saleswoman. I could sell ice to Eskimos, cars to Detroit, and sunscreen to vampires. But even I would struggle to make over $50,000 selling this moth-eaten, dust-smelling, moldy old pile of junk."

"What are we going to do?" asked Samantha.

"I know book burning is wrong," said Nanny Piggins, "but in this instance, some gasoline and a match would be the kindest thing. It would put these painfully boring tomes out of their misery."

"But you promised to run a bookstall," said Michael. "I don't think Headmaster Pimplestock would like it if you just did a bonfire instead."

"You're probably right. He's very inflexible, even for

a headmaster. Never mind, we'll just have to find some good books," said Nanny Piggins. "The kind people actually enjoy reading. And I think I know just where to start."

A few minutes later, they were all standing on the front doorstep of their most unpleasant neighbor, Mrs. McGill, which made the children very anxious.

"Is this safe?" worried Samantha. "You know she complains to the police if we even look over her fence. So what's she going to do if we actually ring her doorbell?"

"Just leave it to me," said Nanny Piggins.

The children did not need to be told. There was no way they would voluntarily speak to their most feared neighbor.

Suddenly an eye appeared at the peephole. "Who is it? What do you want?" demanded Mrs. McGill.

"We want you to give us your extensive collection of romance novels," called Nanny Piggins back through the mail slot.

"But surely Mrs. McGill doesn't read romance novels," whispered Derrick.

"Of course she does," said Nanny Piggins. "All lonely old ladies do. I bet she has a stack of them by her bed at all times."

"I've called the police," shrieked Mrs. McGill through the still-closed door.

"Oh good," said Nanny Piggins happily. "I want to talk to the sergeant about donating some of his books. I bet he's got loads of detective novels."

Suddenly the front door opened a crack, and Mrs. McGill's wizened face appeared. "Why should I give you any of my books?" she asked.

"Because it's easy for you to get them delivered to your house—month after month. But there is no way you can get them out of your house without being seen," said Nanny Piggins. "And if word got out that you secretly read three or four dozen romance novels a month, your image would be ruined."

Mrs. McGill's eyes darted up and down the road, hoping no one had overheard this dreadful thought.

"Children would no longer fear fetching their balls from your garden," continued Nanny Piggins. "Adults wouldn't worry about letting their dogs poop on your lawn. And hoodlums would drop their candy wrappers on your front path."

Mrs. McGill visibly shuddered. She hated hoodlums. And she thought everyone was a hoodlum: the postman, the milkman, even the Meals on Wheels lady.

"You must have piles and piles of books stacked up in your house by now," continued Nanny Piggins. "I bet they reach up to the ceiling. If you don't give them to me, one day soon a stack will collapse on you and you'll suffocate beneath a pile of sweet-dream romance stories."

Mrs. McGill glared at Nanny Piggins. Nanny Piggins glared back. Then Mrs. McGill leaned forward and whispered, "All right, you can have them, but secrecy is of the utmost importance. Bring a truck around to the back of the house at two AM and wear a ski mask." Then Mrs. McGill slammed the door in their faces.

"Wow!" said Derrick.

"You were right," said Samantha in amazement.

"I usually am," said Nanny Piggins.

Just then the Police Sergeant arrived and Nanny

Piggins set to work persuading (harassing) him to donate his mystery books. And so the week progressed. Nanny Piggins forced her way into Headmaster Pimplestock's house and made him give up his cowboy comics (which were all he ever read. He was not a literary man). She got the retired Army Colonel who was secretly in love with her to donate some really exciting war adventure stories. She got Hans the baker to donate cookbooks (the best kind of books after romance novels, in Nanny Piggins's opinion). And she even got Mr. Green to give up his law books (that was easy—she just took them). By the end of the week they had quite a collection.

"Now we've got some books that people will actually want to buy," said Nanny Piggins with satisfaction, "as well as your father's law books, which will be handy if we need to prop up a rickety table."

"But do we have over fifty thousand dollars' worth?" asked Samantha.

"Easily, I should think," said Nanny Piggins (math was not a great strength of hers). "Who needs a Gutenberg Bible when I've got three whole boxes of Regency romances?"

The morning of the school fete arrived. Nanny Piggins, Boris, and the children got there early to set up the stall, only to discover that Headmaster Pimplestock had given them the worst location at the fete. (He could not resist the opportunity to be petty.) They were away from all the other stalls, down a path and around behind the boys' bathroom. But Nanny Piggins was not worried. She assumed the rest of the fete would suffer when all the customers gathered around her stall.

After they had arranged all the books into categories and put up signs saying EVERY BOOK $1 (Nanny Piggins's pricing policy was based on what would involve the least amount of mental arithmetic), they went up the path to check out the rest of the fete.

"I've got a good feeling about this," said Nanny Piggins. "With just the right amount of persuasion, flirting, and ankle biting, I think I can sell all those books."

But as they arrived at the main part of the fete, suddenly a large stall in front of them opened. The canvas awnings that covered the sides dropped to the ground, one at a time, revealing the most spectacularly beautiful stall ever. Every flat surface was entirely covered in cakes, cupcakes, tarts, flans, and pastries. And every treat was beautifully presented on a doily, with a ribbon and a little picture of a kitten or a puppy dog. And flashing Christmas lights twinkled over the cornucopia of cake, making the whole stall look like a magical wonderland of delight.

"Gosh!" said Derrick.

"Crikey!" said Michael.

"Is that honey cake?" said Boris.

Nanny Piggins did not say anything, because standing there in the middle of this astounding display of baked goods was her archrival, Nanny Anne. Nanny Piggins was torn between really wanting to bite her nemesis and really, really wanting to bite into one of the cakes.

"Good morning, Nanny Piggins," smiled Nanny Anne smugly. "I'm so glad you've gone ahead with your stall after all. It's very valiant of you. If you do it again next year, you can go the extra step of putting some thought into your display."

Nanny Piggins's heart sank. She knew she was a brilliant saleswoman and every single book on her stall was an excellent purchase, but why would anyone even glance at her books when only a short walk away was this beautiful gleaming display of delicious delicacies?

"I'm opening the gates!" announced Headmaster Pimplestock.

"Are you ready, Nanny Piggins?" asked Samantha.

"What?" mumbled Nanny Piggins. For once her confidence was actually shaken. "Oh yes, of course." She pulled herself together. "We can do this. True, it does appear that Nanny Anne has ruined our chances with her gaudy display of frippery, but we must push on. After all, we don't know what's going to happen. There could be an earthquake that causes the ground to open up and swallow Nanny Anne's stand, in which case we will be able to draw the customers over to look at our books."

Nanny Piggins, Boris, and the children went back down the path and set to work. And there was soon a crowd. But the problem was that all the people were facing the wrong way. They were a crowd gathered around Nanny Anne's stall who were lined up all the way down the path. As a result, by the end of the first hour of business, the bookstall had only sold seven books.

"Are we near our $50,000 target yet?" asked Nanny Piggins.

"Not quite. We're still $49,993 short," said Derrick.

Nanny Piggins slumped down on a box and silently rubbed her snout. The children did not know what to say. They had never seen their nanny defeated before. But then suddenly Nanny Piggins leaped up and exclaimed, "You stay here!" and she sprinted off through the school gates.

"Do you think she's coming back?" asked Michael.

"Oh yes," said Boris, "although perhaps not today. Today isn't going very well, is it?"

Boris and the children valiantly continued to run the bookstall, but without Nanny Piggins's sales talents (biting people on the leg), they sold even less. They were just considering giving up and going over to Nanny Anne's stall to buy a slice of cake when they heard a car horn honking wildly. They looked up in time to see Mr. Green's Rolls-Royce smashing through the school gates and mowing down Headmaster Pimplestock's shrubbery.

"That can't be Father driving, can it?" exclaimed Samantha.

"No, look! It's Nanny Piggins," cheered Michael.

And sure enough, Nanny Piggins was at the wheel. She yanked on the hand brake, doing a one-hundred-and-eighty-degree spinning skid that brought the car to a halt next to the bookstall.

"Quick, children," ordered Nanny Piggins. "Start unloading."

"What have you got?" asked Boris. "More books?"

"No, better than books—cake!" said Nanny Piggins, opening the trunk to reveal boxes and boxes of home-baked cakes. "I went home and whipped some up. As well as the few dozen I already had stored in my room, you know, for emergencies."

"But we can't sell cake! Nanny Anne is running the cake stall," said Michael.

"Of course we can't. But who's to say we can't strap a slice of cake to every book I sell as a free gift?!" declared Nanny Piggins.

So that is exactly what she did. And, as a sales tactic, it was an immediate success. It is an amazing fact of life that people do not realize how much they would enjoy a romance novel or an alien-abduction thriller until there is a slice of chocolate mud cake tied to its side. Nanny Piggins was soon inundated with customers.

Then, gradually, a strange thing happened. While Nanny Anne's stall sold a lot of cakes, she did not get a lot of repeat business because when the buyers sat down to eat their slice they soon discovered, to their horror, that she had put carrot chunks, or beetroot puree, or sometimes even grated parsnip in it.

Because, you see, Nanny Anne could not help herself. Even when she was running a cake stall, she could not resist the urge to turn every slice into a nutritionally balanced, healthy meal. So when she baked, she used artificial sweetener instead of sugar, low-fat spread instead of butter, and whole-grain flour instead of white flour. As a result, even though her cakes were beautiful on the outside, on the inside they were horrible (not unlike Nanny Anne herself).

Whereas Nanny Piggins's cakes were a delicious symphony of pleasurable delight. (I will not list the ingredients she used because, if I did, Nanny Piggins would hunt me down and bite my leg for giving away

Nanny Piggins was soon inundated
with customers.

her secrets; but suffice it to say, she did not use health foods.) Her customers, even those who had driven long distances to get home before they took a bite, immediately got back in their cars and rushed back to buy more, much more. So much so that Nanny Piggins, Boris, and the children soon ran out of books to strap the cake to. They even used up all the knitting patterns. Boris had to rush home and fetch more of Mr. Green's law books.

By the end of the day Nanny Piggins had just one slice of cake left, from an octuple-chocolate chocolate cake (that is chocolate cake with chocolate chips, chocolate icing, chocolate filling, chocolate cream, and chocolate sprinkles, all sandwiched between two blocks of chocolate). But there were still dozens of hungry customers.

"Who will buy this copy of *Introductory Calculus*, which just happens to come with a free slice of the most chocolatey chocolate cake ever?" asked Nanny Piggins, keeping up the pretense that she was really just selling books.

"Me!" "No, please, me!" "I've got to have it!" exclaimed various members of the crowd.

"All right, the only fair way to settle this is to auction

it off to the highest bidder," announced Nanny Piggins. "Who will open the bidding?"

"One hundred dollars!" screamed a hungry man.

"A thousand dollars!" yelled an even hungrier woman.

"Ten thousand dollars!" called a man so hungry he was prepared to re-mortgage his house.

There were hands flying up left and right as people desperately tried to bid for the cake, because it is in adrenaline-filled moments like these that people see the world with greater clarity. And they realize that there are much more important things than rent payments, bills, and health insurance premiums—namely, cake. Everyone in that cake-frenzied crowd knew that they might never climb Mount Everest or swim the English Channel, but if they just ate this one heavenly slice of octuple-chocolate chocolate cake they would have really achieved something in life.

When the fete closed, Headmaster Pimplestock went around to every stall collecting the cash and thanking the stallholders.

"How did you do this year, Nanny Anne?" simpered Headmaster Pimplestock.

"I've made $8,200," smiled Nanny Anne smugly as she handed over her pink frilly cash box.

"You're such a treasure," gushed Headmaster Pimplestock. "The school is lucky to have you as a member of our community."

Nanny Anne smirked and batted her eyelids at the headmaster (even though she did not have any dust in her eye).

Finally Headmaster Pimplestock walked down the path and around behind the boys' bathroom to the last stall, where Nanny Piggins was waiting.

"Did you manage to get rid of some of those books, then?" asked Headmaster Pimplestock.

"Oh yes," said Nanny Piggins. "We ran out of books two hours ago, which is why I had to break into your storeroom and take all the horrible, miserable novels you hand out as required reading and sell them as well."

"You did what?" blustered Headmaster Pimplestock.

"Which is how we came to make $108,000," said Nanny Piggins, wheeling out a big trash bin full of cash.

(Her cash box had soon overflowed, so Nanny Piggins had to borrow a large trash bin from the janitor to hold her enormous profits.)

Headmaster Pimplestock looked at the huge stash of money. "You haven't robbed a bank, have you?" (He knew Nanny Piggins well.)

"I did consider that," admitted Nanny Piggins. "But the banks aren't open on Saturdays and it would be rude to break their door."

Headmaster Pimplestock did not know what to say. So Boris helped him.

"This is where you say thank you to my sister for all her hard work," said Boris.

Headmaster Pimplestock looked up at the ten-foot-tall bear looming over him and gulped. "Thank you so much for all your hard work, Nanny Piggins."

"And..." prodded Boris.

"What more do you want?" asked Headmaster Pimplestock.

"We want you to promise that you'll go straight home and call the fashion designer," prompted Boris.

"You were serious about that?" asked Headmaster Pimplestock incredulously.

"Oh yes," said Nanny Piggins.

"Very serious," said Boris, leaning in close to Headmaster Pimplestock's face.

"All right, I'll call Milan today," promised Headmaster Pimplestock, reaching for the wheeled trash bin.

"There is one more thing," said Nanny Piggins, not letting go of the bin handle.

"There is?" asked Headmaster Pimplestock worriedly.

"I want to run the cake stall next year," said Nanny Piggins.

"But Nanny Anne—" began Headmaster Pimplestock.

"Only sold $8,200 worth of cake," interrupted Nanny Piggins.

"All right, the job is yours," conceded Headmaster Pimplestock.

"Then here you are," said Nanny Piggins, handing the trash bin to Headmaster Pimplestock, who ran away as fast as a man pushing a very heavy overstuffed trash bin possibly can.

"Well, children," said Nanny Piggins. "I think we have done an excellent day's work."

"We've raised $108,000 for the school," agreed Samantha.

"Fifty-eight thousand of which will be spent on flying in a leading fashion designer to yell at Headmaster Pimplestock in Italian," added Boris.

"But more importantly," said Nanny Piggins, "I have proven, yet again, that my cakes are much, much better than Nanny Anne's."

CHAPTER TEN

Nanny Piggins and the Ominous Sounds

anny Piggins was not having a good day. Now, as you have probably gathered from reading the previous nine chapters, Nanny Piggins had a much higher ratio of good days to bad days than most ordinary people. But even she, occasionally, every year or two, would have a bad day. And this was one of them.

It all started when she tried to get to the sweetshop before closing time. The sweetshop always closed at noon on Sundays so that the man who ran it could have a nap. After all, fulfilling the sugary requirements of the town's children (and Nanny Piggins) all week was exhausting work.

Nanny Piggins, Boris, and the children had set out for the sweetshop in plenty of time, but characteristically, they were distracted along the way. First by an ice-cream truck going in the opposite direction; then by the new slide at the park; then by them all going to the service station to buy a four-liter bottle of motor oil to pour on the slide because Nanny Piggins thought it was not slippery enough.

As a result, when they set out for the sweetshop again, two hours after they had first left the house, they were cutting it a little close. When they rounded the corner, they were horrified to see the sweetshop man hanging the CLOSED sign in his window and pressing the button to lower the heavy security door.

"Noooooo!!!" screamed Nanny Piggins. Dreading the horror of a full Sunday afternoon without chocolate, she immediately sprinted toward the shop. It was an impressive sight. The children knew their nanny could fly when she was blasted out of a cannon, but they never realized she could fly along the ground as well. If the

Olympic one-hundred-meter final had been held in the street in front of the sweetshop that afternoon Nanny Piggins would have definitely won the gold medal. However, as she narrowed the distance between herself and the sweetshop, the security shutter narrowed the distance between itself and the ground.

Fortunately Nanny Piggins had seen many adventure movies, so she knew exactly what to do. Just as the security shutter seemed impossibly close to the pavement, she dived headfirst at the gap, sliding under the shutter, smashing open the shop door with her head, and coming to a halt on the sweetshop floor.

Unfortunately this is where her luck ran out, for Nanny Piggins had slightly misjudged something. Whether it was the hardness of the shop door, the un-slipperiness of the floor (if only the sweetshop man had kept it regularly oiled), or her own height—no one will ever know. One thing was clear, however: Nanny Piggins had not slid into the shop quite far enough. As a result, the shutter continued down and landed on her trotter.

"Owwww!" said Nanny Piggins.

"Oh no!" said the shopkeeper, horrified to see his best customer get crunched by his security door.

"Mmm-mmm-mmm," said Nanny Piggins as she bravely distracted herself from the pain by eating a handful of chocolate bars that happened to be within arm's reach.

An ambulance was called, and Boris and the children rode with Nanny Piggins to the hospital (Boris had to ride on the roof because ambulances are not designed with ten-foot-tall dancing bears in mind). At the emergency room, after numerous X-rays, investigations, and proddings (that only made it hurt more), the brilliant medical minds declared Nanny Piggins's ankle to be sprained. They sent her home with an elastic bandage, a pair of crutches, and instructions to stay off her trotters for a week.

"Hmpf," said Nanny Piggins as Boris carried her up the stairs to her bedroom.

"Is the pain dreadful?" asked Samantha.

"Oh, I don't mind the pain in my trotter. I can ignore that. I'm just upset that I forgot to stock up on supplies while we were at the sweetshop," complained Nanny Piggins.

"There were a lot of distractions," comforted Boris, "what with Michael calling an ambulance, Derrick holding the ice blocks to your foot to stop the swelling, and the shopkeeper weeping and begging forgiveness."

"Well, if the ankle injury doesn't kill me, I may not survive the night because I'll starve from lack of chocolate," said Nanny Piggins.

"You did manage to shove thirty-seven chocolate bars in your pockets while you were lying on the floor of the shop," Samantha reminded her, "and eat them all on the ambulance ride to the hospital."

"Ankle pain makes me hungry," admitted Nanny Piggins.

"Would you like us to go down to the kitchen and bake you some cake," asked Michael, "just so you have basic supplies to see you through?"

"That is very kind," said Nanny Piggins, "but it's all right. I told the sweetshop man to ring Hans at the bakery and he knows what to do—in cases of extreme emergency he is to hire a helicopter and drop a crate of basic rations on our roof. So I shouldn't be surprised if they are there now."

And Hans, being a good baker, had followed those instructions precisely. Unfortunately (as mentioned in Chapter Six), the roof of the Greens' house was not one-hundred-percent structurally sound, so Boris and the children actually found the huge crate of gourmet cakes sitting on top of Mr. Green's dresser, having smashed straight through the roof and into his bedroom (which is a lesson to us all. If you are going to have something dropped onto your home from a helicopter, make sure your roof has sturdy crossbeams).

"Do you think your father will notice the hole?" asked Boris.

"If he does, we could put some plastic wrap over it and tell him it's a skylight," suggested Michael.

Nanny Piggins made it through the night, but the next morning her ankle was not only swollen, it had also turned all the colors of the rainbow. So Boris helped her get settled in a cozy chair by the window, with her trotter propped up on a cushion, and the children made her comfortable by putting a stack of novels within arms' reach on one side and a huge box of chocolate bars (that the sweetshop man had sent over as a get-well present first thing that morning) on the other.

"Would you like me to bring up the television?" asked Boris.

"No, it's all right," said Nanny Piggins. "I've got my binoculars, so I can watch TV through Mrs. Simpson's window. She always watches *The Young and the Irritable* and *The Bold and the Spiteful*, so I won't miss my programs."

"We've got to go to school," said Derrick.

"But you went last week!" complained Nanny Piggins.

"Only on two days," said Samantha.

"Your school is so hypocritical," sighed Nanny Piggins. "The teachers always complain about class sizes, but when I do something to help reduce numbers by keeping you home, they complain about that too."

"Boris will be here to look after you," said Samantha.

"Actually, I can't," said Boris. "I've been hired by the bank to teach their tellers ballet."

"Why?" asked Nanny Piggins. "All they do all day is sit behind a big counter taking people's money."

"Apparently studies have shown that bank tellers are the most miserable human beings on earth. So they are seeing if introducing ballet to their lives cheers them up," explained Boris.

"Now I feel bad about complaining," said Nanny Piggins. "Your day is obviously going to be a lot more painful than mine. I have my novels, my chocolate, and my binoculars. True, I can't perform acrobatics or gymnastics or chase down the ice-cream truck, but at least I will be having fun."

So Nanny Piggins was left on her own. And she was immediately incredibly bored. She tried to ease the boredom by spying on the neighbors with her binoculars, but nobody in the street was doing anything interesting. (Mr. Levinstein was doing his Jazzercise workout in his living room, but Nanny Piggins had seen that many times before, and watching his chubby tummy wobble was not as funny the twenty-seventh time as it was the first.)

Nanny Piggins tried amusing herself with chocolate, but once she had stuffed two dozen chocolate bars in her mouth (three seconds' worth of entertainment), she was left wondering what she could do with the other six and three-quarter hours of the day before the children came home. So she picked up a book.

Samantha had put out a stack of her own favorite kind of novels—girl-detective stories. Nanny Piggins usually preferred romance, but she enjoyed any story that involved excitement, mystery, and completely unqualified amateurs making citizen's arrests, so she was soon engrossed. She avidly read as the girl detective showed up all those silly police officers with their forensic teams, legal procedures, and years of experience, simply by following the clues. Nanny Piggins enjoyed the books so much she even skipped watching *The Young and the Irritable* (confident that Bethany would not actually tell Bridge about her secret marriage to Hutt while suffering amnesia in Nepal, at least not for another six episodes).

So when the children came home from school, they were surprised to find their nanny happily reading her books. In fact, Nanny Piggins was so happy that she had only eaten two dozen of the three dozen cases of chocolate the sweetshop man had sent over—so there was something left for dinner.

The next morning Boris and the children set Nanny Piggins up in her cozy position by the window again.

"Are you going to spend the day reading detective novels again, Nanny Piggins?" asked Derrick.

"Oh, no, I won't have time," said Nanny Piggins. "Today I'm going to fight crime."

"But the doctors said you mustn't move!" protested Samantha.

"I won't have to!" said Nanny Piggins. "In *The Case of the Naughty Math Teacher*, girl-detective Tracey McWeldon was snowbound in her house, but she still solved the case simply by using deductive reasoning and tidbits of information she had picked up while gossiping with her friends on the telephone."

"I thought you'd been put off crime fighting after that trouble with the Neighborhood Watch," said Derrick.

"I'm willing to give it another go," said Nanny Piggins.

"So do you want us to fetch the telephone?" asked Michael.

"Yes, please," said Nanny Piggins. "And the telescope from your father's study. I want to be able to invade the privacy of the people down at the far end of the street as well."

"But what if there isn't anybody in the street committing a crime?" asked Samantha.

"Ha!" laughed Nanny Piggins. "I thought you'd read these books. There is always someone committing a terrible crime right under your nose. It's only because the police aren't as intelligent and observant as a fourteen-year-old girl that they never notice."

So the children went off to school, just as worried about their nanny as they had been the day before, except now for different reasons.

"You don't think she's going to get into trouble, do you?" asked Samantha.

"How much trouble can she get into sitting in a chair in her room?" asked Derrick.

Samantha and Michael looked at Derrick. He blushed. They all realized the answer—a lot.

At first there was no crime for Nanny Piggins to solve. But she kept busy by calling Mrs. Roncoli across the street and telling her the answers to her crossword puzzle (Nanny Piggins was using Mr. Green's powerful telescope to read over Mrs. Roncoli's shoulder as she sat at her kitchen table).

But at ten o'clock Nanny Piggins hit the jackpot. She spotted a disheveled-looking man breaking into the Lau residence across the street. Nanny Piggins was immediately on the phone to Mrs. Lau, who she knew (thanks to the telescope) to be in the upstairs bathroom re-grouting the tiles. Nanny Piggins then called the police, sat back, and watched as Mrs. Lau snuck down the stairs, went into the kitchen, picked up a frying pan, crept into the living room, and hit the burglar hard across the back of the head.

As Nanny Piggins later told the police in her official statement: "How was I to know that Mr. Lau had lost his key and was climbing in through his own window so he could get a nap after a long night working the late shift?"

Mrs. Lau did not mind. She was angry with Mr. Lau about some overzealous pruning he had done on her pear tree, so she was glad of the excuse to punish him. But the Police Sergeant gave Nanny Piggins a lecture about wasting police time and instigating violence. Nanny Piggins was, however, not deterred. In fact it encouraged her. Girl detectives were always told off for wasting police time, right before they uncovered the international ring of wicked thieves. So as soon as the Police Sergeant got back in his patrol car and drove off to the doughnut shop (even being around Nanny Piggins made people want sugary food), she went back to work, on the lookout for crime.

Now you have to understand, Mr. Green had not chosen to live on this street because it was a high-crime area. Most of the residents were every bit as boring as him. So even though she had a vivid imagination and a 20x30 power telescope, Nanny Piggins still struggled to find a crime over the next few hours.

She did consider calling the newspaper to report an outbreak of plague when she saw a rat gnawing at one of Mr. Pieterson's garbage bags. And Nanny Piggins consulted Mr. Green's law books (the ones he forced her

Nanny Piggins still struggled to find a
crime over the next few hours.

to get back after the bookstall) to see if she could have Mrs. Merkel arrested for crimes against food when she saw what her neighbor was cooking for her husband's dinner (but it turns out you can't have someone arrested for bad cooking unless that cooking is so bad it causes injury. So Nanny Piggins would just have to wait until Mr. Merkel got food poisoning the next day).

But then, just after lunch—a family-sized coffee cake and a dozen chocolate bars—Nanny Piggins saw a major crime in progress. She saw Mr. Henderson chasing his wife around the kitchen, hitting her on the back. Nanny Piggins immediately called the police. She was actually on the phone with them when she saw Mr. Henderson grab his wife and shake her. Nanny Piggins was so outraged that, despite her doctor's orders, she got up, hopped over to her dresser, picked up her blowgun, hopped back to the window, and shot Mr. Henderson in the neck with a paralyzing dart (given to her years earlier by a generous South American pygmy who was impressed by her circus performance).

The police arrived moments later (the doughnut shop was just around the corner so the Police Sergeant had not gone far) only to find a distraught Mrs. Henderson wanting to prosecute Nanny Piggins for killing her husband.

As Nanny Piggins was to say later in her official police statement: "How was I to know that Mrs. Henderson was choking on a hazelnut and that Mr. Henderson was simply trying to administer the Heimlich maneuver?"

Once Nanny Piggins had assured Mrs. Henderson that her husband was not dead, he would just be asleep for four or five days, the Police Sergeant banned Nanny Piggins from reporting any more crime for the rest of the day. He even took away her girl-detective novels and gave her a boring police manual titled *How to Be a Good Citizen* to read instead.

Nanny Piggins was very glum as she sat in the big, empty house. She still had two hours until the children came home from school, and goodness knows how long until Boris came home from teaching the bank tellers to dance (he had not returned home until three AM the previous day because the tellers had such bad attitudes. They kept trying to charge him a transaction fee every time he spoke to them). So Nanny Piggins was sitting there eating chocolate and feeling sorry for herself when she heard the front door slam downstairs.

"That's odd," thought Nanny Piggins.

Then she heard a muffled voice and, suddenly, the distinct sound of Mr. Green yelling, "That won't do! That just won't do! I won't stand for it! Do you hear me?!"

Nanny Piggins was intrigued. It was unusual for Mr. Green to be home in the middle of the day, and it was unusual for him to be so assertive. Who could he be yelling at? But just then her thoughts were interrupted by a bloodcurdling feminine scream.

"Yaaaagggghhh!"

Nanny Piggins leaped to her feet. Then the shooting pain in her ankle reminded her that she could not stand, and she fell back down.

"Take that! And that! And that!" yelled Mr. Green, his words punctuated by dull thuds. When the yelling and thudding eventually stopped, Nanny Piggins could hear the sound of Mr. Green breathing heavily. (He was not a man who exercised regularly, because he was rightly embarrassed by his appearance in shorts.)

"Oh no, what have I done?" wailed Mr. Green. "What am I going to do?"

Next Nanny Piggins heard the sound of something being moved about, a few thuds, a whack, a bang, something heavy being dragged along the floor, and then the sound of the front door opening.

Nanny Piggins hobbled to the window, where she saw Mr. Green drag the rolled-up living room rug over to his Rolls-Royce and, with some effort, lift it into the trunk of his car.

"Mr. Green's killed someone!" exclaimed Nanny Piggins. Unfortunately, she had used her last paralyzing dart on Mr. Henderson only that morning, so she had no way of stopping him from getting away. What was she to do? What would Tracey McWeldon, girl detective, do?

When Derrick, Samantha, and Michael returned home from school, they were surprised to discover Nanny Piggins downstairs, sitting in the living room, wearing a smoking jacket and a deerstalker hat.

"Are you all right, Nanny Piggins?" asked Derrick.

"Is there any particular reason you are dressed up as Sherlock Holmes?"

"Oh, *I* have never been better," said Nanny Piggins cryptically. "But someone among us has been a victim of a foul crime."

Crash!—Boris burst in through the back door and slammed through the kitchen and into the living room. "What's going on?!" he demanded. "I got a message down at the dance studio saying that a tanker full of honey had smashed into the house."

"You will have to forgive me. That was merely a pretext to separate you from your students," said Nanny Piggins.

"Nanny Piggins, are we going to have to ban you from reading detective novels?" asked Michael sternly.

Just then they heard the wail of a police siren and the screech of tires as the Police Sergeant pulled up and leaped out of his car.

"Oh no," said Samantha. "You aren't going to be arrested, are you?"

"Don't worry; if you are, we'll come down to the prison and smuggle in cakes hidden inside cakes," promised Derrick.

The Police Sergeant, followed by a young deputy, rushed up the Greens' front steps, and let himself in.

"This had better be good, Nanny Piggins," said the Police Sergeant, "or I'm arresting you for wasting police time."

"Ha," laughed Nanny Piggins. "You'll be pinning a medal on me for doing your job in a minute. Just you wait and see."

"Deputy, make a note," grumbled the Police Sergeant. "This afternoon we must talk to the man at the bookstore about not selling detective novels to anyone who lives in this house."

"When all of you have gathered around, I shall reveal the perpetrator," said Nanny Piggins, twirling an imaginary mustache.

"Perhaps we should call a doctor?" suggested Samantha. "Nanny Piggins is on pain medication for her ankle. They may need to lower the dose."

But before they could call the hospital, someone else burst in through the front door. It was Mr. Green. (Boris immediately put a lampshade on his head to hide.) "Where do I sign? Where do I sign?!" yelled Mr. Green.

"Ah good, we're all here," said Nanny Piggins. "Derrick, bar the doors."

"What's going on?" demanded Mr. Green. "I got a message saying my children had been accepted into a wilderness-survival television show, and if I rushed home to sign the permission slips I wouldn't see them for eight months."

"That was merely my cunning ruse to lure you into my trap," announced Nanny Piggins.

"Oh no, Nanny Piggins, you're not going to be arrested *and* fired, are you?" said Michael resignedly.

"Au contraire; there is a wicked murderer among us, and it is he who shall be arrested and lose his job!" declared Nanny Piggins.

"If you don't explain what you are talking about this second, I am going to get very angry," said the Police Sergeant.

"All right, I will begin. I have gathered you all here because at one fifty-seven PM this afternoon I heard Mr. Green murder a woman with the carpet sweeper in this very room!" proclaimed Nanny Piggins.

Mr. Green sat down and dabbed his forehead. He was not accused of murder every day; at least not on any day in the last two and a half years since his wife died. On that occasion he did have to answer some very sticky questions about how Mrs. Green managed to go missing on a crowded boat under such mysterious circumstances. "I did no such thing," he whimpered.

"Ha!" accused Nanny Piggins. "That's the excuse all murderers use."

The Police Sergeant nodded. She was quite right.

"Do you have any evidence?" asked Derrick. Derrick was not as fond of his father as a son usually is, but that did not mean he wanted his father to rot in jail. Also, having lived in the same house as his father for eleven years, Derrick seriously doubted that Mr. Green was capable of doing anything as interesting as committing murder.

"I heard it with my own ears," explained Nanny Piggins. "At one fifty-six PM I was sitting quietly in my room, on the lookout for criminal activity on the street, when I distinctly heard Mr. Green come home, yell at someone, then beat them repeatedly with a blunt instrument."

Everyone turned to look at Mr. Green. He whimpered again. "There's no proof."

"Ah, that is where you are wrong. You will note," said Nanny Piggins, whipping a telescopic pointer out of her sleeve (her years in the circus had taught her to have props at the ready), "that the red armchair is not where it usually is."

"Gosh! She's right," said Samantha. "The red armchair isn't usually jammed up against the television screen. It's usually over on the other side of the room by the window."

"Derrick, if you move the chair to one side, we will be able to observe more physical evidence," said Nanny Piggins.

Derrick moved the chair, and there in the floorboards were several deep, nasty dents. Everyone gasped.

"Tsk, tsk, tsk," said the Police Sergeant.

"It's going to be a devil of a job to get them out with a disc sander," said the Police Deputy knowledgably. (He was very fond of doing woodwork in his spare time.)

"And, Samantha, if you reach under the sofa, you will find another item of interest. Make sure you use your handkerchief to pick it up. You don't want to smudge the fingerprints," instructed Nanny Piggins.

Samantha reached under the sofa and pulled out a very battered carpet sweeper.

Everyone gasped again.

"That's going to be no good for cleaning floors

anymore," said Boris (even though he was still hidden under the lampshade).

"And finally I draw your attention to the spot on the floor where the Police Sergeant is standing," said Nanny Piggins. "What do you see?"

"Nothing," said the Police Sergeant, looking at the floor beneath his feet.

"Exactly!" said Nanny Piggins triumphantly. "Where is the brand-new hearth rug?!"

Everyone gasped for a third time.

"She's right! Father brought home a new hearth rug last week, and now it's missing!" exclaimed Michael.

"That is because *he*"—Nanny Piggins pointed her trotter dramatically at Mr. Green—"used it to roll up his victim and drag her to his car!"

"Deputy, you'd better get out your handcuffs," said the Police Sergeant.

Mr. Green leaped to his feet. "I can explain," he wailed.

The Deputy crash-tackled him to the ground.

"What are you doing, Deputy?" asked the Police Sergeant.

"I thought he was trying to escape," explained the Deputy.

"You were just trying to get in some rugby practice, weren't you?" chided the Police Sergeant. "All right, sir, if you can explain this damning litany of evidence against you then we'd better have it."

"I didn't murder anyone, I swear. I did put the dents in the floor but only because I saw a cockroach and I used the carpet sweeper to kill it," said Mr. Green.

"Piffle!" said Nanny Piggins. "Look at all the marks on the floor. Why would you beat a cockroach so many times?"

"Because I kept missing," admitted Mr. Green.

"Oh," said Nanny Piggins. This actually made sense. They all knew Mr. Green had terrible hand-eye coordination. "But how do you explain the missing carpet? Why would you roll up the carpet and put it in your trunk if there wasn't a dead body inside?"

"Because there was a dead cockroach squashed into the fibers, so I took it straight to the carpet store to get it cleaned," shuddered Mr. Green. "It was yucky."

"Oh," said Nanny Piggins. "But how do you explain the yelling and the high-pitched feminine scream?"

"That was me," said Mr. Green. "I was yelling at my secretary on the telephone. She was trying to reschedule my haircut appointment from two PM to two fifteen PM. And I wouldn't stand for it. I don't see why I should have to rearrange my day just because my hairdresser has to go to a funeral."

"But, sir, the high-pitched feminine scream?" asked the Police Sergeant.

"I don't know what you're talking about. The pig must have been hearing things," said Mr. Green shiftily.

"Sir," reproached the Police Sergeant.

"All right, all right," burst out Mr. Green. "I admit it! The cockroach ran up my leg, and I panicked—I took my trousers off. But at that very moment a woman collecting for the Salvation Army came to the door. And when she saw me through the window in my underwear, she screamed."

"Preposterous! You'll never be able to prove that," scoffed Nanny Piggins.

"Well, actually I can," said Mr. Green sheepishly, as he opened a drawer in the sideboard and took out a Salvation Army collection tin. "She dropped this as she ran away."

"You were going to hand that in, weren't you, sir?" said the Police Sergeant sternly.

"Oh yes," lied Mr. Green.

And so, while the abandoned collection tin proved that Mr. Green was morally bankrupt, it also proved that he was innocent of the charge of murder.

"Oh dear," said the Police Sergeant. "I'm sorry, Nanny Piggins, I think I really will have to arrest you for wasting police time this time."

But just then the doorbell rang, and the man from the carpet shop came in. "We got all the cockroach goo out of your carpet, Mr. Green," he said as he unrolled the rug on the floor.

Now it was the Police Sergeant and the Deputy's turn to gasp.

"Get out your handcuffs, Deputy, it looks like we're going to arrest Mr. Green after all," announced the Police Sergeant.

"What? What for?" asked Mr. Green, desperately trying to guess which one of the many not-quite-legal things he did in his daily life as a tax lawyer that the Police Sergeant might be arresting him for.

"That is the famous Great Luxor Carpet from the Highcrest Mansion that was stolen last week. So either you are a cat burglar or you have received stolen property," accused the Police Sergeant.

"It was a gift from a client," protested Mr. Green.

"Why would a client give you one of the most valuable handmade Persian rugs in the entire world?" asked the Police Sergeant.

"He was a friend?" suggested Mr. Green.

"Sir," chided the Police Sergeant.

"It was a reward for helping him set up an offshore truffle-trading scheme for funneling money out of the country," blurted Mr. Green, "which technically is not in any way illegal. I know because I had my clerk triple-check the law books."

"Deputy, get out your notepad. Okay, Mr. Green, tell us, which client? What was his name?" ordered the Police Sergeant.

Mr. Green gulped. But he did as he was told. Much as he hated losing a client to the prison system, he much preferred that to having to spend time in the prison system himself.

And so, just as she had predicted, Nanny Piggins managed to use her recuperation time to foil a gang of wicked international thieves, which just goes to show, if you set yourself goals, you can achieve anything. But Boris and the children were relieved a few days later when Nanny Piggins was able to start walking again, so she could return her energy to being the world's most glamorous flying pig/nanny, and leave the girl-detective work to the likes of Tracey McWeldon.

CHAPTER ELEVEN

Nanny Piggins and the Evil Boarding School

Nanny Piggins and the children were sitting around the dining table having breakfast when Mr. Green came in carrying the mail.

"There's one for you," he grumbled as he disrespectfully dumped an envelope in front of Nanny Piggins.

"I wonder what it could be?" said Nanny Piggins. "I hope it isn't the government again. They are always begging me to become an international super-spy, and

I just don't have the time. International intrigue doesn't stop once a day for *The Young and the Irritable*, and I do."

Nanny Piggins tore open the envelope and was immediately surprised. "Leaping Lamingtons!!!" she exclaimed.

"What is it?" asked Derrick.

"If you're going to become a super-spy, can we come too?" asked Michael.

"No, it's better than that," explained Nanny Piggins. "It's a letter from the mayor. They are giving away free chocolate at Town Hall this morning between eight forty-six and eight fifty-two AM."

"That's awfully specific," said Samantha.

"Who are we to question free chocolate?" declared Nanny Piggins. "We must go."

"But we have to go to school," said Derrick, while jerking his head meaningfully in the direction of his father to remind Nanny Piggins that Mr. Green was still sitting at the table.

"Oh," said Nanny Piggins. "Perhaps your father will give you permission to take the morning off?" Nanny Piggins knew there was no chance of this, but she thought it was worth asking, just on the off chance that Mr. Green had a brain lapse and agreed.

"I certainly will not," growled Mr. Green, not even bothering to take the newspaper away from in front of his face.

"Never mind. You go, Nanny Piggins," said Samantha. "You can tell us all about it when we get back."

"And take a suitcase!" suggested Michael. "That way you can bring lots home."

"Good thinking," agreed Nanny Piggins. "Now, what is the time?"

They all turned to look at the clock. It was 8:39.

"Oh dear," said Nanny Piggins. "I don't see how I can send you all off on the school bus and still make it to Town Hall in time."

"I'll see the children off," said Mr. Green.

Nanny Piggins and the children turned and stared at him in astonishment. Rather, they stared at the back of his newspaper because he still had not put it aside.

"You'll do wh—?" began Nanny Piggins.

But then Derrick grabbed her hand. "Don't question it, Nanny Piggins. Just grab the opportunity. Find the biggest suitcase in the house and run like the wind!"

Nanny Piggins did not need to be told twice. In less than three seconds, she was out of the house and sprinting down the street with her circus trunk, a giant suitcase, and the biggest Tupperware container from the kitchen.

When she returned twenty minutes later, Nanny Piggins was a less-than-happy pig. Instead of sprinting, she trudged, and instead of carrying her containers, she dragged them. And not because they were heavy, but because she was heavy of heart. There had been no free chocolate at Town Hall. The doors were not even open. Nanny Piggins had to kick them in with her trotter, which was not easy given that they were the type of heavy two-hundred-year-old antique doors especially designed to stop angry peasants from kicking them down and demanding their taxes back.

Inside, Nanny Piggins had not discovered the mountains of free chocolate described in her letter. There was just a group of old ladies studying Ancient Greek as part of the council's Leisure Learning program. Even after Nanny Piggins had shaken the Ancient Greek instructor by the collar for a full five minutes, she had not been able to uncover the location of the free chocolate. So she came home a very sad pig.

But as she turned the corner onto the Greens' street, she was soon jolted out of her dejection by the most shocking sight. There, on the sidewalk, stood Mr. Green with a very large woman (who, if not for the dress, could easily have been mistaken for a rugby player) and three trunks. And alongside them was parked a school bus. But not the children's regular school bus. This bus was a regal purple and had the words DAMPWORTHINGTON'S BOARDING SCHOOL painted on the side. But most significantly of all, Nanny Piggins could see, beating on the Plexiglas rear window, the fists of Derrick, Samantha, and Michael as they called out to their beloved nanny, "Nanny Piggins! Help us, please!"

Nanny Piggins dropped her trunk, suitcase, and Tupperware and ran toward them. "What are you doing with the children?" demanded Nanny Piggins.

"Just sending them to school," said Mr. Green smugly.

"Yes, but which school?" asked Nanny Piggins.

"I have been fortunate enough to win three scholarships

to an exclusive boarding school," said Mr. Green. (He was very proud of himself. Mr. Green had won the B. J. Silverman Scholarship. It was awarded to the employee at his law firm who used the least amount of stationery five years in a row. Mr. Green had been trying to win this scholarship since Derrick was born, but it was only in the last five years that he had devised his brilliant strategy. At night, after all the normal people in the office went home, Mr. Green went around taking stationery off other people's desks and putting it back in the cabinet. So the stationery tally actually had him in credit, having put back one thousand eighty-six more packets of Post-It notes than he took out.)

"Boarding school? How could you?" asked Nanny Piggins, bewildered that a father could be so heartless.

"At boarding school, they will have all their needs taken care of," said Mr. Green, "and by proper staff. Not pigs."

Nanny Piggins gasped. "That's the real reason, isn't it? You're sending your children away just because you don't want me—the world's most glamorous flying pig—living in your house!"

"I don't have to answer your questions anymore," pouted Mr. Green. "You're fired."

"What?" demanded Nanny Piggins. She had been fired out of a cannon many, many times. But she had never been fired from a job before.

"Fired!" said Mr. Green with finality.

Fortunately the words Nanny Piggins now yelled at Mr. Green were drowned out by the sound of Derrick, Samantha, and Michael pummeling their fists on the bus window, so I will not have to repeat them here in print. Suffice it to say that Nanny Piggins let Mr. Green have a piece of her mind using the type of colorful language you can only pick up from years of working in a traveling circus.

"That's enough of that, then," said the large woman, clapping her hands for silence. "As headmistress of Dampworthington's Boarding School, I won't stand for any shilly-shallying, dilly-dallying, or flibberty-jibbeting. You are not the legal guardian of these children; Mr. Green is, and he has signed them over to me. And I refuse to have any dealings with you. Bruno, our bus driver, has packed your belongings."

Nanny Piggins looked around to see all her things strewn across the Greens' front garden. Someone had obviously thrown them out her bedroom window.

"I suggest you pick them up and go back to the sty you came from," said the headmistress before she turned away and got on the bus herself.

Mr. Green smirked a gloating smile. "Did you enjoy your *free* chocolate?"

Nanny Piggins gasped. "The mayor didn't write that letter at all! You did!" she accused. "It's bad enough to send your children away to endure years of certain misery. But forging a letter that falsely claims the presence of free chocolate! Can you sink any lower?!"

Nanny Piggins was now so angry that Mr. Green became scared. He ran back into the house and locked the new locks (which he had had installed while she was down at Town Hall).

The engine of the bus started up.

"Nanny Piggins?" pleaded the Green children, their faces and hands pressed against the bus window.

"Can't you do something?" asked Derrick, his voice pitifully muffled by the thick glass.

"I'm afraid your father is your legal guardian," said

Nanny Piggins, "and unlike the time he tried to sell you as apprentice sumo wrestlers, sending you to boarding school is technically allowed under the law."

Nanny Piggins reached up with her trotter (which was not easy because she was only four feet tall) and touched each of the children's faces (or rather the places on the bus window the children's faces were pressed against). Nanny Piggins was glad Boris was not there to see this pitiful sight. He would be distraught enough when he heard about it.

As the bus pulled away and she watched the children's faces disappear into the distance, Nanny Piggins wondered if she had Russian blood herself, because she was weeping harder than she had ever wept before. She could not believe it. After all they had been through together, it had come to this. She was never going to see the children again. And she had not even been allowed to give them a hug good-bye.

As they pulled in through the wrought-iron gates, Derrick, Samantha, and Michael were soon to discover that

Dampworthington's Boarding School was ten times more awful than they had imagined it would be. And they imagined something pretty bad because they had read a lot of novels about poor orphans being sent to horrible cheap boarding schools and catching terrible respiratory illnesses.

The boarding school was miles and miles away from anything, out in the middle of the country, presumably to discourage anyone except children with advanced wilderness skills from running away. The building was cold and bleak. The founder of the school had specifically set down in the school's constitution that no heating system was ever to be installed because he believed a child's brain worked best at thirty-eight degrees Fahrenheit. Unfortunately, while the brain may flourish at that temperature, the little fingers, toes, and noses of small children do not. As a result, the entire student body spent nine months of the year huddling. The other three months of the year they sweltered because the founder also believed that fresh air was too much of a distraction, so he had all of the windows nailed shut.

The teachers were unspeakably horrible. We all know what teachers are like at an ordinary school. But imagine the type of teacher who can only get a job at an unheated boarding school in the middle of nowhere. They were not happy, well-adjusted souls. And as one selfish misery guts once famously said, "A problem shared is a problem halved." And the teachers at Dampworthington's believed in this theory wholeheartedly. They spent all day every day halving their own misery by inflicting the other half on the young charges in their care.

Things did not start well for Derrick, Samantha, and Michael. Headmistress Butterstrode (for that was the large woman's name) marched them off the bus, forced them to put on horrible uniforms, and then made them line up in the lobby.

"There will be no more crying," she announced. "Self-indulgent extremes of emotion are strictly forbidden under article one hundred fifty-six of Dampworthington's school rules. And while crying over lost pigs is not specifically covered by the rules, it is, nonetheless, pitiful and shameful, and if I catch any of you doing it again, you will be punished."

"How?" asked Derrick. He personally did not think he could make it through twenty-four hours without shedding a tear for Nanny Piggins, so he was curious to know what would happen.

"Silence!" said Headmistress Butterstrode. "The asking of questions is strictly forbidden under article two hundred twelve of Dampworthington's school rules."

Samantha sobbed.

"No sobbing," said Headmistress Butterstrode. "Sobbing falls under the definition of crying, according to clarifying clause six of article one hundred fifty-six. There are one thousand three hundred and four school rules, a copy of which you will find on your pillows. And I expect you to have them all memorized by nine AM tomorrow. Do I make myself clear?"

"Y—" began the children.

"Shhh!" said Headmistress Butterstrode. "The answering of rhetorical questions is forbidden, under rule eight hundred and three. Do you understand?"

The children did not want to do the wrong thing, but they did not know how to respond when asked a question and then told not to answer it. So they glanced at one another.

"A-a-a!" scolded Headmistress Butterstrode. "Looking at one another when a teacher is talking is not allowed. Rule three."

The Green children, not knowing what else to do, stared straight forward with blank expressions on their faces.

"That's better." Headmistress Butterstrode smiled. "Now. The student body is gathered for lunch. Follow me."

She pushed open a double door and led the Greens into an enormous room full of two hundred children eating in total silence. It really was extraordinary. It was one thing to see a group of two hundred children not talking, but to see them all eating without making any noise—no chewing sounds, no clinking of cutlery, no sipping of drinks. It was eerie to behold.

Headmistress Butterstrode led Derrick, Samantha, and Michael to a platform at the head of the room. "You will now introduce yourselves to the school. You, girl, go first." She gave Samantha a small shove in the back.

Now, as you know, Samantha was a girl who worried a lot. And of all the things in the world she worried about, being forced to do public speaking was one of the worst. In her mind public speaking was right up there with wrestling tigers or swimming with sharks as one of the most horrifically frightening things you could possibly do.

With Nanny Piggins's loving encouragement, Samantha had done many daring things she never imagined herself capable of. But right at this moment, Nanny Piggins was not there, so Samantha did not feel loved nor safe. She felt awful. She had a great big lump in her throat the size of a grapefruit, and a bucket-load of tears welled up behind each eye ready to burst out. Samantha did not think she could say something as simple as "please pass the salt" without falling on the floor, wailing loudly, and beating the ground with her fists. So the idea of being forced to make an impromptu speech was horrifying.

"What should I say?" whispered Samantha hoarsely.

"Your name and a little bit about yourself," said the headmistress.

Samantha stepped forward. All the children in the hall silently put down their cutlery and turned to face her. Samantha considered running from the room, but her legs felt like jelly and she did not think she would get very far. "My name..." she croaked.

"Louder," said Headmistress Butterstrode.

"My name is Samantha Green," said Samantha, "and I..." Samantha paused. She did not know how to describe herself. She had no hobbies. She had no talents. The only thing she had in her life was the world's most glamorous and amazing nanny who led them all on the most astounding adventures on a daily basis (which surely was more than enough for any child). But Samantha instinctively knew the headmistress would not want her to mention that. "I—" continued Samantha. Then she spat out the first thing that came into her mind—"really like chocolate."

Everyone in the dining room laughed.

"No laughing!" snapped Headmistress Butterstrode. "You are all violating the strict 'no mirth' rule of the Dampworthington Code. As punishment, there will be no more food today."

The children all hung their heads and looked at the plates that they had just been forbidden to eat from. But some of them still smiled. Just the thought of chocolate had been enough to cheer them up in such a bleak place.

The rest of the day did not go well for the Green children. Before he was allowed to attend any class,

Derrick was marched off to see the school barber and forced to have a haircut. Derrick tried explaining that he just wanted a little off the sides, not realizing that the school barber was completely deaf and only capable of one type of haircut. (His main job was trimming the school hedges, and they were viciously overpruned.) Derrick emerged from the room with his head completely shaved around the sides and back, and nothing but a short spiky strip of hair along the top of his head. And he had lots of tiny pieces of toilet paper stuck to his scalp where the barber had nicked him with what Derrick was sure was a pair of pruning shears.

Michael fared even worse. A no-food diet did not agree with him at all. When he could not indulge in his favorite hobby—eating treats under a bush in the garden—he became delirious. And in his case, delirium caused him to start telling the truth. He staggered from class to class muttering things like: "This school is simply dreadful," "I really, really hate it here," and "I do miss my nanny, Nanny Piggins." So it was only a matter of time before he found out what the official school punishment was. He was marched out into the school playground, sticky-taped to the flagpole in the center of the quad, and left there in the rain.

Derrick longed to go and rescue his brother, but he was being punished by his science teacher, who had locked him in the chemical closet for not knowing the atomic weight of Rutherfordium.

When the children trudged to their dormitory that night they were exhausted—physically from all the punishment and emotionally from missing their nanny.

"Should we try to run away?" asked Samantha.

"I can't. I don't have the energy," said Michael, flopping on the floor beside his bed. (Students were not allowed to sleep on their beds because that made the sheets untidy. They had to sleep on the cold floorboards next to their beds, because, according to the late Mr. Dampworthington, "shivering was good for the brain.")

"And I don't know where we could run to," added Derrick. "If we went home, Father would only force us to come back. We could run away to sea to become pirates, but I don't know where you go to apply for a position."

"I can't believe I've got to spend nine years here until

I turn eighteen. And poor Michael will have to be here for eleven years," said Samantha.

"Oh, I won't be here that long," whimpered Michael. "I'll probably die of starvation before the end of the week."

"Let's sleep on it. Perhaps we'll think of something in the morning," said Derrick.

So they all went to bed, although none of them slept (not even Michael) because the floor was uncomfortable and their thoughts of life without Nanny Piggins were more uncomfortable still.

The next morning at breakfast, Derrick, Samantha, and Michael were feeling very dispirited as they ate their porridge (the most dispiriting of all breakfast foods) when the meal was interrupted by the main doors from the lobby swinging open. The Green children did not turn to look. They had read the school rules the night before, so they knew that to do so would violate rule 612—the strict "no looking" rule of the Damp-worthington Code. But they heard Headmistress Butterstrode striding toward the stage and a lighter pair of footsteps behind her.

"Children," addressed Headmistress Butterstrode. "We have another new pupil."

The Green children along with the rest of the student body were now allowed to turn and look. Headmistress Butterstrode stepped back, and a girl wearing the Dampworthington school uniform came forward.

"Tell everyone your name and a little bit about yourself," ordered Headmistress Butterstrode.

The girl stepped to the front of the stage. She was not very tall, no more than four feet. She had long fire-engine-red hair and thick black-framed glasses. But, unlike the rest of the school population, she managed to make the uniform look somehow elegant. She scanned the room and fixed her gaze on Derrick, Samantha, and Michael. Then, amazingly, she raised her heavy glasses and winked at them.

The Green children gasped. It was no girl! It was Nanny Piggins!

"Good morning," said Nanny Piggins to the entire school. "My name is Matahari Curruthers-Dingleberry, and I look forward to my time here at Dampworthington's."

She then winked at the Greens again and allowed herself to be led away by Headmistress Butterstrode.

"Nanny Piggins has come to rescue us!" whispered Derrick.

"But how?" whispered Samantha.

"She'll think of something," said Michael.

When Derrick arrived at his French class Nanny Piggins was already sitting in the front row.

"Bonjour, Derrick," said Nanny Piggins with a smile.

"Bonjour, Mademoiselle Matahari Curruthers-Dingleberry," replied Derrick. He wanted to say, "We've missed you so much. How are you going to rescue us? Are we going to dig an escape tunnel? Do you know anyone who can forge passports? Do you have any chocolate?" but he could not, because Derrick was not very good at French so he did not know the words for *missed*, *rescue*, *escape*, *tunnel*, *forge*, or *chocolate*, which is a shame because they are some of the most important words to know in any language.

Nanny Piggins, on the other hand, spoke fluent French. Indeed, her vocabulary was much more extensive than the teacher's, because she knew the type of salty words that would make a sailor blush, and she proceeded to teach them to the whole class.

By exactly copying Nanny Piggins's intonation, the students were soon telling their teacher, with perfect Parisian accents, that his "hair looked like a baboon's toothbrush" and his "breath smelled like a three-week-old Camembert cheese."

The French teacher was deeply offended. (He thought his aftershave, Eau de Cheese, smelled nice.) So Nanny Piggins was soon thrown out of his class and demoted down to Samantha's grade, where she joined their home economics lesson.

When Nanny Piggins saw the spinach quiche the students were being taught how to make, she was horrified.

"Quick, throw them out the window," Nanny Piggins urged her fellow students when the teacher turned her back.

"But what about our grades?" worried Samantha.

"Forget the grades," said Nanny Piggins. "There are much worse things than getting a zero on an assignment, like being forced to eat a spinach quiche."

The students saw the wisdom in Nanny Piggins's words and hurled their classwork out the second-story window (much to the chagrin of the sports class doing sit-ups immediately below).

And so, even before lunchtime, Nanny Piggins was demoted to Michael's class, where they were studying art.

"Today we will be studying the Flemish masters," said the art teacher as he set up an overhead projector (always a sure sign that a very boring lesson is about to follow).

"I'd rather study Jackson Pollock," declared Nanny Piggins.

"Who?" asked Michael.

"He was a brilliant artist who discovered that idiots would pay millions of dollars if he spattered paint about and generally made as much mess as possible," explained Nanny Piggins.

"Abstract expressionism is not about making as much mess as possible," contradicted the art teacher.

"Really? So if I picked up this five-liter bottle of red paint and splashed it all around the room like this..." said Nanny Piggins as she squirted huge splatters of paint across the walls, floor, and ceiling, "that's not abstract expressionism?"

And so Nanny Piggins was soon sitting on the Naughty Bench outside the headmistress's office.

"Do you think she is going to be all right?" worried Samantha. "What if the headmistress sticky-tapes Nanny Piggins to the flagpole?"

"Hah!" scoffed Michael. "I'd be more worried for the flagpole."

"She hasn't even tried to rescue us yet," said Samantha.

"She seems to be having too much fun annoying all the teachers," said Derrick, "but I'm sure Nanny Piggins will get around to it."

And Derrick was quite right. The children had only been sitting in their next class for three minutes when suddenly the fire alarm went off, and a voice crackled over the school's public address system: "Students of Dampworthington's, this is Matahari Curruthers-Dingleberry speaking. I have locked your horrible headmistress in the attic. My real name is Nanny Piggins, and I am here to set you free from this brutal regime. I suggest you rise up and capture all your teachers now. If you hold them still, I will come around to each of the classrooms and help you tie them up."

The student body did not hesitate for an instant. They lunged at their teachers. Some of them had been students at the school for many years, so they had a lot of pent-up emotions to express. And they did not need Nanny Piggins's help. Using their belts, school ties, and ribbons, they had every member of staff tied up in the school gymnasium in less than five minutes.

In the melee, Derrick, Samantha, and Michael found one another, then went in search of Nanny Piggins. They bumped into her just as she was dragging Bruno the bus driver into the gym.

"Nanny Piggins!" exclaimed Samantha.

None of them said any more. They were too busy hugging.

"Um, excuse me," said one of the older students politely, not wanting to interrupt the hug.

"Yes," said Nanny Piggins, looking up, but not letting go of Derrick, Samantha, and Michael.

"What do we do now?" asked the student.

Nanny Piggins looked at the group of two hundred huddled children, all as gray as their school uniforms. "Isn't it obvious?"

"Don't ask them rhetorical questions. They aren't allowed to answer," explained Derrick.

"We must raid the kitchens!" announced Nanny Piggins.

So Nanny Piggins led the children hollering and cheering down to the school kitchen, where they broke open the door and burst into the pantry. The hilarity immediately stopped. There was nothing in the pantry except two hundred industrial-sized boxes of porridge, one hundred loaves of stale brown bread, and three hundred cabbages.

"What is the meaning of this?" asked Nanny Piggins. "Where's all the food?"

"That *is* all the food," explained Samantha. "That's all they feed us here."

"Diabolical!" exclaimed Nanny Piggins. "But never fear; I will soon find you some real food to eat."

Nanny Piggins held her snout high and sniffed about. She quickly latched on to a scent. "Follow me, this way," she said. And so all two hundred students followed Nanny Piggins as she sniffed her way along the corridor, down a staircase, around a bend, and into the east wing of the building. There Nanny Piggins's snout led them to the farthest room, where no student had ever been before—the staff common room.

"We're not meant to go in there," warned Samantha.

"Good," said Nanny Piggins. "If we are all going to be expelled we might as well do a thorough job of it." And she pushed open the door. But the children were too stunned to enter. The staff common room was the most opulent room they had ever seen. There were leather recliners, three-inch-deep wool carpets, central heating, huge wide-screen TVs, and silver platters loaded high with chocolate and sweets of every variety.

"Wow!" said Michael, which perfectly summed up what they were all thinking.

The children were too astonished to know how to react. Fortunately Nanny Piggins was there to guide them. "Dig in," she instructed.

The children were too stunned to know how
to react. Fortunately Nanny Piggins was
there to guide them. "Dig in," she instructed.

The children surged forward and started scoffing. Apart from the chocolate and sweets, Michael (who had a talent for finding forbidden food) also found a giant refrigerator hidden behind a secret panel in the wall, and it was crammed with every flavor of ice cream known to man. So the children chomped, licked, and munched away happily for hours.

The student body of Dampworthington's had just reached the happy point of having eaten so much they felt too ill to even move when Headmistress Butterstrode (slightly disheveled from having had to bite her way out of the jump ropes Nanny Piggins had tied her up with) appeared in the doorway.

"Out! Out, all of you. You filthy, greedy ingrates— out of this common room and assemble in the quad immediately!" she yelled slightly hysterically.

The children scurried as quickly as their swollen stomachs would allow them, out into the quad where they stood in perfectly formed lines with their heads hung in shame.

"You have all been very naughty," scolded Headmistress Butterstrode, "but you, Matahari Curruthers-Dingleberry, have been unforgivable. As such, I have called the school authorities and they will be arriving shortly to prescribe the appropriate punishment."

"Expulsion?" asked Nanny Piggins hopefully.

"Oh, no," said Headmistress Butterstrode. "No student is ever expelled from Dampworthington's. That would be a reward. And we do not reward students here. We punish them."

Derrick, Samantha, and Michael began to worry. Perhaps their nanny's plan was not as well-thought-out as they had assumed.

Just then a black car turned into the school's driveway.

"Aha," said Headmistress Butterstrode. "You are in real trouble now. That is the School District Superintendent. He'll be dealing with you personally."

"I'm sorry?" asked Nanny Piggins. "Did you say you called in the District Superintendent?"

"Yes, I did," said Headmistress Butterstrode. "I bet you're feeling sorry now."

"Well, this is going to be interesting," said Nanny Piggins.

The black car pulled up next to the quad, the door opened, and the District Superintendent stepped out. The Green children immediately recognized the plump elderly man. He was the same School District Superintendent who had inspected their old school when Nanny Piggins had been headmistress for the day. The same superintendent who had fallen deeply in love with her.

"Superintendent," said Nanny Piggins as she whipped off her red wig and thick glasses and dazzled the Superintendent with her most winning smile.

"Headmistress Piggins!" said the Superintendent breathlessly. During the months that had passed, the Superintendent had convinced himself he was over his infatuation with the world's most glamorous flying pig, but as soon as he saw her he realized he was not.

Headmistress Butterstrode stared in openmouthed shock as the Superintendent rushed forward to kiss Nanny Piggins on the trotter, gushing, "Oh, I've missed you. I've missed you so."

Suffice it to say, the meeting in the school office that followed did not go as Headmistress Butterstrode had expected. After two hours of discussion, the Superintendent, accompanied by Nanny Piggins and Headmistress Butterstrode, emerged to address the school.

"I have been informed by Headmis...I mean, *Nanny*

298

Piggins, of all that has gone on at this school—" began the Superintendent.

"But she's just a pig," protested Headmistress Butter-strode.

"I'll have none of that," snapped the Superintendent. (He could be quite masterful when he wanted to be.) "I will not allow you to malign such a fine lady."

Nanny Piggins smiled.

"As such, I have decided to follow Nanny Piggins's recommendation and close this school immediately," said the Superintendent.

The entire student body erupted in cheers.

"All the teachers will be fired..." continued the Superintendent.

The students cheered again.

"And I ordered a team of bulldozers to come and demolish the school building in less than an hour," concluded the Superintendent.

The students did not think they could be any happier. But just then a truck pulled into the school's driveway.

"That truck looks familiar," said Derrick.

"It should," said Nanny Piggins.

It was Hans the baker's truck being driven by Boris.

"I called Boris and told him to bring supplies. If we are going to have a demolition party, it would be rude not to provide refreshments," explained Nanny Piggins.

Much, much later that night, Nanny Piggins, Boris, and the children returned home to the Green house. When he heard them come in, Mr. Green did not protest or question them. He stayed hidden in his office. You see, getting rid of his children had not brought Mr. Green the relief he had expected. As soon as he had the house to himself, Mr. Green had known it was too good to be true and that his luck could not last. If anything, it was a relief just to have the children back and let things return to normal, and not to be attacked by a vengeful Nanny Piggins as he had expected. (Little did he realize that Nanny Piggins had a long memory and fully intended to exact revenge at a later date.)

"Are you happy to be home, Nanny Piggins?" asked Samantha.

"Oh yes," said Nanny Piggins. "Sleeping in Boris's

shed was all right for one night. But I much prefer being here with my whole family."

To celebrate, Nanny Piggins asked Boris to bake a great big chocolate cake. She would have made it herself, but she did not want to stop hugging the children, not just yet.

Nanny Piggins's World-Beating Cake Recipe

The Boris

(Chocolate soufflé with a piece of honeycomb stabbed in the center)

This is the dessert Nanny Piggins and Michael invent in Chapter Eight of *Nanny Piggins and the Runaway Lion*.

Soufflé has a reputation for being very difficult and tricky to cook. This is not at all true. Soufflé is only difficult if you cook it for a dinner party and the guests ruin your preparations by ringing the doorbell or trying to talk to you or get you to make eye contact with them.

If you do what Nanny Piggins does and cook soufflé as an afternoon snack when there are no distracting guests to bother you, or pesky vegetables or soup courses to cook at the same time, then you won't have any difficulties.

If you have a social disposition and insist on friends coming to visit, then Nanny Piggins recommends not inviting them to dinner. Instead, invite them to watch you cook and eat a soufflé. The result will be much more educational for them and satisfying for you.

If your guests complain of hunger, you can order a pizza, but only after the soufflé has been given the proper respect and attention it deserves.

Ingredients

6 eggs

1 pound dark chocolate

3 tablespoons powdered sugar

1 piece honeycomb (or even better, chocolate-covered honeycomb)

1 very large box of assorted chocolates

1 responsible adult

Directions

1. Capture a responsible adult (preferably one with advanced circus training, but any trustworthy person over the age of twenty-one will do). They will be in charge of operating the oven, handling hot things, and dialing 911 if they accidentally hurt themselves because they are not paying close enough attention.

2. Butter an appropriate-sized oven dish (about six inches in diameter) and place it on a metal baking tray.

3. Preheat the oven to 375 degrees Fahrenheit.

4. Separate the eggs so that you have six egg whites in one bowl and four egg yolks in another bowl. (You will have two egg yolks left over. You can give these to someone making an egg-white omelet to make it taste better.)

5. Break up the dark chocolate into a bowl and then soften it in the microwave. (How long this will take depends on your microwave, so do it cautiously the first time, in forty-second blasts on a medium setting.)

6. The assorted chocolates are essential at this stage. Open the box and start eating them liberally to prevent yourself from eating the soufflé ingredients.

7. Whisk the egg yolks.

8. Mix the melted chocolate with a wooden spoon until smooth.

9. Combine the chocolate with the egg yolks.

10. Whisk the egg whites until they reach soft

peaks, add the sugar, and keep whisking until the egg whites reach stiff peaks. Once they reach stiff peaks—stop! Don't overwhisk them. (If you accidentally overwhisk them, don't panic; just add another egg white and carefully whisk in.)

11. Now pour the chocolate and yolk mixture onto the egg whites and fold it in carefully with a wooden spoon. You want to retain as many air bubbles as possible. So don't worry if there are a couple of unmixed patches.

12. Pour into the buttered oven dish.

13. Pick up the tray with the dish and put it in the oven.

14. Bake for twenty-five minutes.

15. As soon as it comes out of the oven, stab a piece of honeycomb into the center, preferably chocolate-covered honeycomb. Then serve (or eat it yourself).